WILL
ON THE
INSIDE

ANDREW ELIOPULOS

WILL
ON THE
INSIDE

Quill Tree Books
An Imprint of HarperCollinsPublishers

Quill Tree Books is an imprint of HarperCollins Publishers.

Will on the Inside
Copyright © 2023 by Andrew Eliopulos
All rights reserved. Printed in the United States of America.
No part of this book may be used or reproduced in any manner
whatsoever without written permission except in the case of
brief quotations embodied in critical articles and reviews. For
information address HarperCollins Children's Books, a division of
HarperCollins Publishers, 195 Broadway, New York, NY 10007.
www.harpercollinschildrens.com

ISBN 978-0-06-322870-2

Typography by David Curtis
23 24 25 26 27 LBC 5 4 3 2 1

First Edition

To you. Yes, you.
You are not alone.

WILL
ON THE
INSIDE

1

AS GROSS AS IT SOUNDS

You know that expression "there's no *I* in *team*"?

Coaches always say it when they want you to work together. Or else when they want you to stop showing off.

When it comes to soccer, my best friend, Henry, can't help showing off. For one thing, he's really good. Like, he once pulled off an actual bicycle kick—*in a game*. Can you imagine?

That was when we were on an academy team together. Some guys on that team even started calling him "Legs." That's how epic the kick was.

Anyway, forget Henry for a second. What I wanted to say is, when you think about it, "there's no *I* in *team*" is kind of, almost, sort of a threat. It's at least a warning.

How many times have I been on a team where someone didn't fit in? And not like Henry, who somehow manages to stand out *and* fit in at the same time, by being so cool that everyone else wants to be like him.

No. I mean like Justin Kemp from that same academy team. In practices, Justin would cry if he got hit with the ball, until the very guys who came up with "Legs" started calling Justin "Kemp the Wimp." Justin didn't last until the end-of-season banquet. He left the team and joined his school's math club instead.

Or like Francis Redmond, who was the other sixth grader to make it onto the Oakwood school team last year, along with Henry, my friend Luca, and me. On the very first day of practice, Francis came out in these rainbow socks, and when the older guys asked why he was wearing them, he said it was because he was bi. He just said it. Like . . . wow.

I won't repeat what the guys called Francis. But anyway, he didn't last a week. He didn't just leave the soccer team, either. He switched to private school. Even though it was midway through the school year.

You see what I mean?

No *I*'s allowed.

There's been a lot on my mind lately, but somehow that's the thing I can't stop thinking about as my parents drive me to the hospital to get my procedure.

The procedure I'm having is called a colonoscopy, and it's as gross as it sounds. But even though I'm nervous about what my new doctor might find when she sees the results, I'm even more nervous about what the guys would say if they knew I was having a . . . a *colon*oscopy. They know I'm headed to the hospital but that's it.

What nicknames would they come up with for me if they heard the whole story?

I don't know what I'd do if I couldn't play soccer. My family would never pay for private school. And I'm definitely not joining any math clubs, either. That's like going to school after school.

"All right, champ," my dad says, pulling into the parking lot of a hospital so large, I can't even see the whole thing from the car. "You ready for this?"

Am I ready for this? I'm definitely ready for it to be over so life can go back to normal, but I'm not sure if that's the same thing.

"I guess so," I say.

"Everything's going to be fine," my mom says. I think

she needs to hear that as much as I do. There's no way my parents would've *both* taken off work to bring me here if they weren't nervous, too.

"Okay, then," my dad says. "Let's rock and roll."

2

HEAVY ARTILLERY

The good news is, for a colonoscopy they put you to sleep with anesthesia, so you don't have to feel it. Anesthesia sleep is not like regular sleep, though. It falls faster and heavier. When I wake up, it takes me a minute to figure out I'm not dreaming.

My vision is narrow and wobbly, for one thing. And this isn't the room where I fell asleep. But even as this new room begins to take shape, what really trips me up is the snow outside my window.

Here's what you have to understand: I live in Georgia. We hardly ever get snow—not even over winter break. I didn't think it was possible for it to snow in April, and unless I've been asleep for a very long time, that's the month we're in now. The championship tournament starts at the end of next week, and after the tournament it's practically the end of the school year.

That's just it, though. The way my head feels, I can't be totally sure when *or* where I am, or if any of what I'm seeing is even real.

"Will? Sweetie? You awake?"

My mom's voice. It's real. That's when I know the rest of it is, too.

Mom's in a chair beside my bed, clutching a blanket that's gotten much bigger since she picked up knitting it again this morning. My dad is pacing at the far end of the room, his face pressed close to his phone. Whatever he's reading has him worried or mad—maybe both.

I try to say a few different words at once, and what comes out is a garbled mash-up that must sound like a zombie groaning his way back from the dead.

Suddenly the room becomes a flurry of words and movement. "I'll go let the nurse know," Dad says, rushing out into the hall, while Mom leans in and asks, "How do you feel, sweetie? Do you need anything?"

I shake my head.

What I mean is: I don't know.

I don't think the anesthesia has worn off all the way yet. My eyes can hardly stay open, and when I try to move my head, the whole room sways.

I start to regain the feeling in the rest of my body. It's weird; it's like my stomach is full and empty at the same time. Or like I have to go to the bathroom. But that can't be true, because I haven't eaten anything in more than a day.

My stomach makes a weird rumbling sound, like it knows I'm thinking about it. Even though it's just my mom and me in here, it's kind of embarrassing.

Then Dad returns, followed by a nurse in purple scrubs. I'm pretty sure she said her name was Sylvie, but that was right before they put the anesthesia in my IV. I was a little distracted.

"Hi there, Will," I-think-Sylvie says. "I brought you some cookies and apple juice. I'm going to put them right here for you, and Dr. Clarkson will be in soon."

My parents exchange a lightning-fast look, as if I won't see it. I know what they're thinking. They're thinking that when Dr. Clarkson comes back, it could be with the answer to what's been wrong with me this year.

For the record, I'm definitely thinking about this,

too. It's just that I'm so hungry all of a sudden. It's hard to think about anything besides these cookies, which I devour in four bites.

"When we're done here," Dad says, "we can go get a milkshake at McDonald's. How does that sound?"

"Sounds good," I say, even though I've never liked their milkshakes as much as Dad and my sister, Lexie, do. They act like McDonald's milkshakes are in a class of their own, which is funny, because Lexie works at a place in the old Main Street shopping center called Scoops and Shakes, where the milkshakes are so good they're right there in the name. They have this chocolate and marshmallow one that tastes like an actual s'more, even down to the smoke from the fire. I've always thought McDonald's shakes taste like cold, sugary air.

"Let's wait to hear from Dr. Clarkson," Mom says. "She might not want him eating any dairy for a while."

"Oh, right," Dad says. "I forgot. In that case, maybe we can make him some mashed potatoes and chicken noodle soup when we get home."

This is one of many things I've gotten used to in the past couple months: my mom and dad having a conversation that's more *about* me than *with* me. Shortly after soccer season "kicked off" (har har), I started coming home from practice feeling tired and queasy. Not normal tired, either. Like, face-planting-on-my-bed tired. Full-body exhaustion. I'd head straight to the bathroom, and from there I'd hear my parents calling out from one side of the house to the other—"Again today?" "He looked even paler than last time!"—and on and on, like I wasn't even there.

It finally got to the point where they made me go see Dr. Yi, who's been my doctor since I was a baby. She still gives me stickers when I visit. A little weird, sure, but I feel safe with her.

Then, two weeks ago, Dr. Yi told me that I had to go see a specialist in Atlanta named Dr. Clarkson, and Dr. Clarkson wanted me to come in for a colonoscopy "sooner rather than later." That's when it finally sank in that I might not just be tired from a stomach bug.

That I might have something wrong with me for real.

"Sweetie?" Mom says now, seeing that I'm halfway dozing off again. "We have something for you, if you want it. We were saving it until you were fully awake."

She folds up the blanket and sets it down beside her, then digs around in her canvas tote bag. Finally, she comes out with a big brown envelope that has my name on it, written very small in pen.

Mom and Dad watch me expectantly as I peel back the seal and remove a giant piece of construction paper, folded in half. On the outside of the paper, it says GET WELL SOON, and underneath that: MR. DYSON'S WEEKEND WARRIORS.

Mr. Dyson leads the middle school Bible study class at my church every Sunday. Weekend Warriors is the name all of us in the class chose for ourselves at the beginning of the year.

Inside the card, it looks like everyone from the group has written me a note or signed their name. Henry, Zander, Yasmin, Madison. Even the sixth graders I don't really talk to that much. They've all written that they're praying for me. That they hope this latest test will finally help me feel better.

"Wasn't that nice of them?" Mom asks.

"You've got a lot of fans and admirers, champ," Dad says.

But the truth of it is, I suddenly feel weird. I hate the idea of everyone knowing I'm sick. The thought of them taking a break from this week's class, focusing all their attention on me? That kind of attention makes me nervous.

Still, I nod.

"Very nice," I say.

"Knock, knock," says Dr. Clarkson at the door, and instantly, my parents go stony-faced and silent. I am definitely awake now.

Dr. Clarkson is shorter than I am, and she has a kind smile, but somehow she manages to be intimidating at the same time. Maybe it's the official white coat she wears, or the way all the nurses and hospital workers talk to her really fast, like they know she's busy.

"How are we feeling, Will?" she says, stepping over to the end of my bed.

"He just woke up," Dad says.

"We were giving him his card from his friends at church," Mom adds.

Dr. Clarkson smiles at them, but then she turns right back to me, still awaiting my answer.

"I'm okay," I say.

She nods. "Well, thank you for doing such a great job on your prep," she says, referring to the disgusting stuff I had to drink last night to make me go to the bathroom.

My system had to be clear so they could see it with their camera. That's the "scope" in colonoscopy. "I know that's no fun."

I shrug. Dr. Clarkson watches me for another moment, in case there's something more I want to say.

Finally, she continues. "Okay, McKeachie family. The good news is that the scopes did give us a solution to our mystery. Is it okay if I share this information with everyone at once?"

"Please," Dad says, while Mom just nods. I guess it wasn't a question for me.

"Well, we'll need to wait until the biopsy results come back to confirm, but based on the pattern of inflammation I'm seeing, it looks like we're dealing with Crohn's disease here."

My dad lets out a little noise, like the start of a "no" that got stuck on the runway. My mom grips her blanket so tightly her knuckles go white.

Crohn's disease was one of the possibilities Dr. Yi had mentioned. She tried to put an upbeat spin on it, but it sounded pretty scary—especially after we did some more reading on the computer at home.

We came across a lot of conflicting information, but one thing every article agreed on was that Crohn's disease has no cure. At least not yet.

"Now, the really good news is that we caught this early," Dr. Clarkson continues. "We all owe Dr. Yi a big thank-you for spotting the signs and not waiting another moment to get the tests underway."

The hairs on my arm prickle at that. If this is how it feels to catch this early—the exhaustion and the stomach pains that feel like running cramps at best and having a screwdriver stabbed into your guts at worst—I'd hate to think what it would've meant to catch it late.

"What's the plan from here?" Mom says, in her problem-solver voice. Mom manages inventory for a big craft supply store. She sounds like this whenever a shipment goes wrong.

Dr. Clarkson says, "Well, I'd like to get Will started on some medicines right away. Will, I know you're probably still woozy from the anesthesia, so I'm going to write everything down for you to look at more at home. But the main thing to mention while we're all here together is that I plan to put you on a couple different medicines, including a steroid called prednisone, to help your body fight the inflammation and heal. By starting with the heavy artillery, we can take advantage of this early diagnosis to get a jump on the disease. Our goal is to get you into remission in no time."

My head is spinning.

Inflammation? Remission? Heavy artillery?

I know all these words—separately, mostly—but I'm having a hard time following what they all mean when you put them together. I don't know what they mean when they're all about *me*.

My dad is hung up on another word.

"A steroid?" he says. "You mean, like, a *steroid* steroid?" He flexes his arm to illustrate the kind he means.

"Oh, no," Dr. Clarkson says. "This is a corticosteroid, used to lower Will's immune system response. With auto-immune disorders like Crohn's disease, it's an overactive immune system that's causing the inflammation. You're thinking of anabolic steroids."

"Well, good thing our Will is just fine with the muscles he already has. Isn't that right, Will?" Dad gives my leg a shake. "I bet you're going to be MVP in the game against

Gordon. They're not going to know what hit 'em."

Dr. Clarkson winces, and even before she speaks, I already know what she's going to say.

"That's the bad news. Once Will is in a good remission, he should be able to get back out onto the field with no problem. There've been a number of professional athletes with Crohn's disease, in fact. When it's under control, there's not much you can't do."

"But when it's not under control?" Mom says.

"Well, you tell us, Will," Dr. Clarkson says. "How has it been so far this season?"

She gestures to her stomach as she says this, as if I need a reminder of where the problem is (I couldn't forget if I tried).

"It's been okay," I say.

"You *have* been going to the bathroom a lot," Dad says. "Do you ever have to do that during practice?"

"I mean, once or twice . . ."

"And do you have any stomach pains?" Dr. Clarkson asks. "Part of my worry is the level of contact in soccer. If you run into another player or get hit in the stomach with a ball, it could be fine, or it could make your symptoms worse. We want to make sure your body has a chance to heal."

I think of practice last week, when Kent kicked a ball so hard it probably would have circled the Earth if my body hadn't been there to stop it. It took the wind out of me, and it definitely stung for a minute after that, but that shot would have hurt anyone. Right?

"I don't know," I say.

Dad frowns. "I know you don't want to hear this, champ, but I think you're better safe than sorry."

Of course Dad would say this. He works for an insurance company, the same one where my grandpa worked. Being safe, not sorry, is basically his whole job.

"Can we talk about it more at home?" I say, not wanting to make a scene.

"No, I think it's better to discuss it here, while we have Dr. Clarkson to help," Mom says.

Dad nods. "Your health is the top priority. Plus, if you're out there on the field and give it anything less than your best, you're never going to be happy with yourself afterward."

That hits home. The stomach pains and the frequent

trips to the bathroom are annoying, but I've been able to live with them so far. The real problem has been that bone-tired feeling, like after practice I can't take another step.

It's not just after practice, either. We run laps around the field to start out every day, and at our first couple practices, I ran all four up near the front of the pack, with Henry and Luca. Then it reached a point where just getting to the end of the fourth lap felt like a marathon-level achievement.

That's how I knew I needed to see Dr. Yi in the first place.

If this steroid will help me get my energy back, so I can play like I used to, then I guess it's worth waiting. The last thing I want is to hurt the team in the championship tournament.

Dr. Clarkson looks sympathetic. "Truly, once this flare-up is under control, and we've got you in a good remission, you can get right back out there. I've had patients play basketball, baseball, golf, you name it."

Coach Yosef always tells us about the power of positive thinking, and how soccer and endurance are mental games as much as physical ones. For months, I'd been trying to push through the exhaustion and make my body work harder, like I could do it if I just wanted it enough. When Dr. Yi told me it wasn't my fault I couldn't do it, honestly, it was a relief.

But now, I'm glad to have a doctor who believes in the power of positive thinking, too. It's like Dr. Clarkson is my personal trainer, an all-new coach here to tell me how we're going to win in overtime.

Only the other team is my own body. So maybe not the best comparison after all.

"How long does the pred . . . steroid . . . take to work?" I ask.

"You should feel at least a little better in a matter of days," Dr. Clarkson says. "And you call me right away if you don't. Any amount of time feeling bad is too long to feel bad."

Any amount of time feeling bad is too long to feel bad.

The words make me feel better already. And if I keep feeling better—in a matter of days, like Dr. Clarkson says—I'll be able to play in the championship tournament, no problem.

I look down at the card from the Weekend Warriors.

I look out the window at the impossible snow.

I guess a lot of things seem impossible until they are actually happening. And if getting an incurable disease seemed impossible a year ago, maybe next year I'll be saying the same thing about how fast I got better.

I guess the list of what's impossible gets a little smaller every day.

3

PLAY IT COOL

When Mom drops me off for my first day back at Oakwood, everyone on the quad stares at me like I'm a celebrity, or maybe a new species of bug that's been caught in a jar.

I guess all it takes to get famous around here is missing three days of school in a row.

I did end up posting about my diagnosis on my feed, not because I really wanted to, but because my teammates were all messaging to ask how I was. I figured it was easier to say I had a . . . a *disease* . . . Well, to say that once, instead of a dozen different times. The last thing I wanted was to repeat the same sob story over and over, like some kind of bad-news robot.

Will. Not. Well.

Dad emailed the school, and then he convinced me it was a good idea for him to call Coach Yosef separately, so he'd know to prep an alternate for the Gordon game. I didn't get around to mentioning that part in my post. I guess deep down I still didn't want it to be true.

The problem is, now I don't know who knows what. *Somebody* must've spread the word, because my feed is set to private—it's just my friends—but random people keep stopping me on my way to first period.

They all want to know: "How are you, Will?"

I'm not even sure where to start.

I'm glad that my science teacher, Ms. Calhoun, seems to have gotten the full story. When everyone starts crowding around my desk before the bell, she comes to my rescue right away.

"All right, class, let's give Will some breathing room."

She gives me a reassuring smile, like she can tell I'm shaken up. Maybe she knows I hate being the center of attention. Whenever I get called on in class—or worse, whenever I have to stand in front of the room, like for a presentation or something—I can feel my heart squeeze up and my hands go cold. That's been the case for as long as I can remember. Maybe I'm not as good at hiding it as I thought.

Now that I think of it, though, the worst side effect, the stomach cramping, only started more recently. I guess that could be another Crohn's disease thing.

"Jarrod and Seema, can Will join your group for the last part of the lab this morning?"

My classmates nod, their eyes darting my way when they think I won't notice. Who knows what they've heard? Maybe they think I'm contagious.

I haven't even had a chance to look at my makeup work from this week, so unless this lab is about corticosteroids, I don't think I'm going to be much help to the group.

My sister, Lexie, loves to give me a hard time about how all my friends are soccer friends. I think it's because, for some weird reason, she's never really liked Henry that much, and he's the one who got me into soccer in the first place. She says I need to branch out—that no one should have only one type of friend. I say she needs to mind her own business.

Anyway, it's not true. I have more than one type of friend. Like Yasmin from Weekend Warriors. She doesn't play soccer. Granted, she doesn't go to Oakwood either, so

I don't really see her except at church. Still, she counts.

What Lexie doesn't get is, it's easier to make friends with somebody when you're on a team with them. She's never liked sports, so I wouldn't expect her to understand. But if you keep your head down and play your position well, a team is basically a built-in friend group.

Plus, when I'm out on the soccer field, it doesn't matter how many people are on the sidelines watching, I don't get any of my usual spotlight jitters. I feel invisible.

I feel invincible.

I try to channel that invincible feeling in the lead-up to lunch, as math, English, and Spanish all play out exactly the way science did. It's like that nightmare where everybody's pointing and laughing at you, plus that other nightmare where you forgot to study for a test. It's a nightmare squared.

Finally, when my class is dismissed to go to the cafeteria, I spot Henry in the hallway at the same moment he spots me, and the way he shouts *"Will!"* like he's so excited to see me, even though I was only out for three days, makes me feel a million times better.

"Dude, how you feeling? I saw your post."

"Yeah, not one of my favorite weeks so far, not going to

lie," I say. "Did you hear anything else? Like from Coach?"

"You mean how you can't play in the Gordon game? Yeah, Coach told us at practice. But don't even worry about it. That sixth grader Amit stepped in for you at center midfielder, and he's actually pretty good. Not as good as you," Henry quickly adds, noticing my frown, "but good enough that we should still get the W, no problem."

"Sweet," I say, even though it stings a little that it took all of one practice to replace me. Center midfielder is *my* position. The one I've played on every team I've ever been on.

"My dad says you started taking steroids. You Hulking out yet?"

Henry's question catches me off guard. How would his dad already know about what medicines I'm taking?

Unless . . . oh.

Henry's dad must have seen my dad at church last night. Dad went to Wednesday worship while Mom and I stayed home. We ate (my millionth bowl of) chicken noodle soup and watched our favorite show, *Simon Says Danger*.

It makes me feel weird to picture all the adults talking about me at church, when I wasn't there. It's not like my disease or my medicine are secrets. It's just . . . This feels like another way of being in the spotlight, and for something I definitely didn't want.

"It's not the Hulking-out kind of steroid," I finally tell Henry.

"Dude, every steroid is the Hulking-out kind. Just wait. One day, when you least expect it, you're going to get into a fight, and the roid rage is going to come out, like, *rrraaawwwrrr.*"

Henry makes a dinosaur claw with his hand as he roars. The joke is that I would never get into a fight, and we both know it. At least I think it's a joke. Dr. Clarkson certainly didn't say anything about roid rage.

We get to our usual lunch table, where Luca and some of the other guys from the team are already sitting. Besides Henry, Luca is my closest friend, and it's been that way ever since the three of us made the school soccer team last year. We were the only sixth graders to make the cut, not counting Francis Redmond and his rainbow socks.

It's not totally equal, though, because I've known Henry a lot longer than I've known Luca. Henry and I go to the same church. We were even in our church's preschool together, and that's when Henry got me into soccer. Luca and I only started hanging out last year.

If it feels unequal to Henry, too, he's never said. But Henry makes new friends the way trees make oxygen from carbon dioxide. I make friends the way trees do everything else.

Today, Luca starts frowning as soon as he sees me.

"Hey, Will. Sorry about your disease. That sucks, dude."

"It is what it is," I say, repeating a phrase my dad uses whenever something sad but predictable happens, which is pretty often in the insurance business.

"I bet Coach will let you be the ball boy or manager or something until you can play again, so you can still ride the bus with us to the away games."

"Yeah, you *have* to come to the games, Will," Henry says. "You're like our mascot. Or our good-luck charm."

Ball boy? Mascot? The last thing I want is to be a *mascot*. Our mascot at Oakwood is—wait for it—an acorn. It's a constant source of jokes at our school, since mascots are supposed to be fearsome animals, like cougars or cheetahs. Not nuts with swoosh lines to make them look like they're moving fast.

Not kids who are too sick to play, either.

"Actually, it sounds like I'll only have to sit out the one game next week," I say. "And the Gordon game's at home. So we're all good."

Henry and Luca exchange a look that says they don't believe me, but they don't know how to say it.

"Seriously," I insist. "My doctor said this medicine will only take a few days to kick in."

"Okay," Henry says, like he's trying to buy time. "Except . . . my dad said . . ." He turns to Luca for help.

"Just come talk to Coach," Luca says. "Better to have a back-up plan, right? Worst-case scenario?"

"If you say so," I reply. It does feel good to know it matters to them that I come to the games. It makes up for the fact that they've clearly been talking about me, based on whatever Henry's dad heard, I guess from my dad. "Do you think I could get a ride home with you after practice, though?" I ask Henry. "I was supposed to take the bus today because my parents work till practice is over. If I try to change plans now, they'll definitely say no."

"Of course, dude," Henry says. "My mom loves you. She won't mind."

"Oh, speaking of love!" Luca says, only realizing how loud he just was when a few of the other guys look our way. Luca smiles innocently and waits until they go back to their business, then leans in like he has a big secret to share. "Will, did Henry tell you what happened while you were out?"

"Luca," Henry says in a warning voice, and I get a prickly feeling at the back of my neck. Henry never keeps secrets. If he doesn't want to share, he probably has a good reason.

I shrug, but Luca can hardly wait to get it out, he's so excited.

He whispers, "Griffin Miller asked Henry to go to the spring dance with him."

The prickly feeling morphs into full-on chills.

This is what I was trying to say about Luca before. Why I'm slow to make friends.

This is the kind of moment where I have to admit Lexie has a point, when she says I need to branch out.

I try to play it cool. Keep my answer short and vanilla, as if I don't care.

"Yeah?" I say.

"For real," Luca says. "I'm not even messing with you."

If there was a silver lining to all the hospital stuff this week, it's that—in all honesty—the spring dance had fallen off my radar for one peaceful minute there. I didn't even go to the dance last year, because the sixth graders have their own separate one, and everybody said it was a waste of time. I was sort of hoping I could skip it again this year, even if the dance for seventh and eighth graders is supposed to be a whole thing.

Maybe Crohn's disease is just the excuse I was looking for. Maybe that's silver lining number two.

I can tell from the look on Luca's face that he's still waiting for me to have a bigger reaction. Meanwhile, Henry just looks miserable.

"Weren't you planning to go to the dance with Julie?" I ask Henry.

"See?" Henry says to Luca. Then to me he adds, "Thank you."

"Sure, sure, but does *Julie* know that?" Luca says, like he's really loving this. "Last I heard, you still hadn't asked her. And that was yesterday after school."

Henry's ears go a little pink. "Stop playing, Luca. You know I'm just figuring out the best time to do it."

"Well, you better stop waiting around, is all I'm saying." Luca grins. "Who knows who else might ask you if you don't?"

I really should let the conversation end there. It's clear Luca is ready to move on, and I'm so ready to stop talking about this with him.

But it's like I can't help myself. Like my mouth moves faster than my brain.

In a whisper, I say to Henry, "Why do you think Griffin asked *you*, though?"

"I don't know," he replies. Then he lowers his voice again. "Maybe he's gay?"

Luca laughs like this is the funniest thing. "Uh, you think, Sherlock?"

Henry has reached his limit now. He rolls his eyes. "Whatever, Luca. It's not like you have a date, either. You're only jealous no one would ever ask *you* to the dance." It's a burn so epic it finally shuts Luca down.

But me?

I can still feel my heart beating hard enough that I swear the guys must be able to hear it.

Because for one brief second there, even though it made no sense, I thought Luca was telling me that Griffin Miller had asked Henry to the dance, and that—as impossible as April snow in Georgia—Henry had said yes. And in that moment, I felt exactly like I did when I got slammed in the stomach with a soccer ball last week.

It was like I felt . . . jealous. So jealous it was painful. I'm sure Henry and Luca could have seen it if they'd been paying attention.

Jealous of Henry? Jealous of Griffin?

Jealous of I don't even know how to say it, exactly. I guess it's this: If any boy could go to the Oakwood spring dance with another boy and get away with it, it's Henry. Nobody gives Henry a hard time for long. He shrugs off that kind of stuff like it's nothing, and he always gets the last word in a throwdown.

That's not me, though.

There's no way I could ever go to a dance with a boy. Not at this school. Even if I wanted to. Even if . . . No way.

If Griffin had asked me, I wouldn't have even *told* Luca about it.

Just thinking about that now makes my stomach hurt. Bad.

"Hey, uh, I just remembered I'm supposed to go talk to Mr. Hayward before class," I say, scrambling to get up from the table so I can make it to a bathroom before I'm sick.

"You want me to come with?" Henry asks.

I shake my head, then hurry away before he can insist.

Is this a Crohn's disease thing or a regular nerves thing?

Does it make a difference?

4

THE COWARDLY LION

I've never exchanged more than a few words with Griffin Miller, but I remember exactly what the few words were.

It was April of last year. The championship tournament was over (we were out after the second round), and the drama club was doing *The Wizard of Oz*. Even though my friends and I weren't planning to go see it, Principal Baylor thought it was so good that he asked the drama club to perform it *during* the school day one Friday. Attendance was mandatory.

Luca was bored out of his skull, but Henry seemed to be loving it, to the point where I wondered why he hadn't just gone to see it one night.

I had to admit I was super impressed, too. The stage

in our auditorium-slash-gym is tiny, but the cast was doing all these complicated dance moves, and some of the actors were really funny.

Griffin Miller was especially funny. He was playing the Cowardly Lion, but I kept thinking about how brave he had to be to get up in front of the whole school in that huge furry costume and make his voice sound like a cat coughing up a furball. Especially as a sixth grader.

Henry acts goofy like that sometimes when we're all hanging out, but I've been in English class with him before, and even his voice goes flat when he has to read aloud. Playing somebody else is hard work.

When the cast came out for the curtain call, Griffin took off his big lion head and held it under his arm. We'd had a couple classes together in the fall, so I knew who he was by that point in the year. But it's like I was actually seeing him for real for the first time. He was *in his element* on that stage.

That's what my dad always says about me and soccer— that even when Henry and I joined our first team, playing in the six-and-under rec leagues where all the little kids just run from one end of the field to the other, tripping over the ball, it was easy to see me on the field and know that I was "in my element."

I always liked the idea of that, like I was born to play soccer. Like it's part of who I am. I've never been the best player on any of my teams (that honor usually goes to Henry, although last year there was an eighth grader on the school team who outclassed him), but I've always felt like I loved playing soccer the most out of anyone. It makes me happy that my dad can see that about me, just from watching me on the field.

That day in the gym, I thought Griffin Miller was both in his element *and* the best actor on stage. He was great, and he enjoyed it. That's a powerful combination.

Anyway, when the curtain call ended, there were still ten minutes before the final afternoon bell rang, so the teachers just let us all hang out and talk. I had to run to the bathroom, but right as I was coming out, Griffin and some of his castmates were headed in, probably to wash off their makeup and change out of their costumes.

There was a split second when Griffin and I made eye contact, and even though I never do this, because I'm really shy around people I don't know, I said, "Hey—good job," and actually held up my hand for a high five. That's what we do at the end of every soccer game: everyone on our team gets in a line, and everyone on the other team gets in a line, and the two lines walk past each other, everyone giving high fives to everyone else. It was an instinct, I guess.

Griffin said, "Hey—thanks," and gave me a high five right back.

And that was it. That was the whole interaction.

For the rest of the school year—all four weeks of it—I kept wondering if I would run into Griffin again. I imagined what I might say if I saw him. Maybe I'd ball my hands into fists and say, "Put 'em up, put 'em up," which is one of the Cowardly Lion's funniest lines in the play. But that sounded dumb, even in my head. And I didn't run into Griffin anyway. Not even on the last day of school, which is basically a free-for-all outside.

And then it was summer, and I more or less stopped thinking about him.

But Luca's story has me thinking about him again.

I guess Griffin Miller is even braver than I realized.

5

THE FREQUENCY ILLUSION

After school, I head to the locker room with the other guys. I even change into my soccer clothes, minus the shin guards and cleats, and I throw on a hoodie because I know it'll be colder on the field if I'm not playing. I wonder if Coach would still make me run laps if I'm temporary team manager. If not, that's the best argument for being temporary team manager I've come up with so far.

The energy in the locker room is as rowdy as ever. Thankfully, the guys don't bother me with questions like so many of my classmates did, probably because they already know what's up.

But when I walk over to the side office just off the

locker room, where Coach Yosef is gathering his clipboard and gear, he seems surprised to see me in the doorway.

"McKeachie," he says, because he calls us all by our last names, "how you feeling?"

"I'm all right," I say.

"That's good to hear, son. Really good to hear. So what can I do for you?"

I try to keep my voice down, because I don't want the other guys to hear me ask what feels like a pretty embarrassing question.

"I was talking to Henry and Luca at lunch, and they said, I mean, since I can't play right now, maybe I could be team manager or something? So I can stick with the team?"

"Say that again, son? You gotta speak up. It's noisy in here," Coach says.

He says this loudly enough that a few people perk up behind me and pay attention, even while they act like they're still rummaging in their bags or their lockers. I can feel their ears on us.

"I was just saying, could I be team manager until I can play again? I can help with the equipment and stuff."

"Yeah, Coach," Henry says, stepping into the doorway

beside me. "Then Will can still ride the bus with us to the away games."

I don't even bother to remind him that I'm planning to be back on the field before the next away game. I can tell by the look on Coach's face that it's a lost cause either way.

"Sorry, boys, but I have strict orders from Will's dad, who's just following the doctor's advice. Until you're feeling better, I can't let you near the field, in case you get hurt."

"I thought I just wasn't supposed to *play*," I say, hating how tiny my voice sounds.

"I can't have you out there, Will. It's a liability, and it's not worth risking your health just to get a front-row seat to the games. I'm really sorry. You know I'll be the first person to throw you a party when you're feeling better and can rejoin the team."

Rejoin the team. I know he probably doesn't mean it like that, but it sounds like Coach is saying I'm *off* the team now. Henry bucks up like he wants to argue some more, but I stop him with a look. I didn't feel great about this idea to begin with, and at this point, it's all just making me feel worse.

I shuffle out of the locker room, trying to keep a low profile. I swear that Amit, the guy who took my place at center midfielder, is watching me and looking a little relieved to see me go. His brand-new position is safe.

I don't even try my parents, since they're still at work. Instead, I text Lexie, thankfully catching her just as she's leaving school, about ten minutes away. Lexie has work today, too, so I know she's probably annoyed about picking me up, but she and my parents have been acting extra nice to me this week, after the hospital. Plus, I'm sure if she tells her boss at Scoops and Shakes that she's late because of me, it'll be fine.

I make my way to the pickup area in the quad in front of the school. There are still some people out here waiting on their parents; mostly they stand in groups or sit together in circles, playing phone games and stuff. But there's one guy standing off on his own, listening to headphones and bouncing his head along to the beat. His hair is almost entirely brown like mine, but in the very front, he has a bright blond streak that curves up in a wave. He has a smile like he just remembered something funny, and he's had that smile every time I've seen him.

Griffin Miller.

Lexie was telling me the other day about this thing called the frequency illusion that she learned about in her

AP Psychology class. It's where you hear about something new and then immediately think you see it everywhere, when the truth is, you're just *noticing* it more, now that you're in the know.

I've been thinking about the frequency illusion these past couple days, ever since my diagnosis. Now that I *know* I have Crohn's disease, I'm seeing new signs of it everywhere, including that rumble in my stomach whenever I'm the least bit nervous. Honestly, it's like I can't *stop* thinking about what's going on in my stomach, and that never used to be the case before.

I guess now I'm also experiencing the frequency illusion *about* the frequency illusion. Because here's Griffin Miller, right after we were talking about him at lunch. Maybe I *have* been seeing him around school, and I just wasn't paying enough attention.

I stand in the only open spot in the pickup area, which is close enough to Griffin that I can sort of hear the music in his ears. It sounds electronic, all thumps and noise.

Am I nervous, or is my stomach starting to hurt again?

Frequency or illusion?

"Hey," I hear.

Not an illusion: Griffin Miller has removed one of his

headphones, and he's talking to me.

"You're Will, right?" he asks.

I glance behind me, as if there could be another Will he's talking to. Really, I'm checking to see if anyone else is watching us. I know Henry and Luca are at soccer, but still. It's like part of me thinks one of them could come running out at any moment, maybe to bring me something I forgot in the locker room. What would they say if they saw me talking to Griffin Miller after what Luca told me? What would they call me then?

No one's there.

I face Griffin and nod.

"I heard you were in the hospital," he says. "That must have been scary."

You'd think at this point in the day, I'd be used to everybody knowing my business. But nope.

If anything, the bug-in-a-jar feeling only got worse as the day went on, like somebody forgot to poke holes in the lid and I almost ran out of oxygen.

I take a deep breath.

I start to respond, *It is what it is*, like I have all day.

But that's not how I really feel, is it?

"It *was* scary," I admit. "I'm just glad it's over."

"My cousin Kayla had to get her appendix removed, and she was in pain for like a week afterward."

"Ouch," I say.

"Yeah. She's totally fine now, though. She's in veterinary school."

"Cool."

I realize I'm fidgeting with the strings on my hoodie. I try to put my hands in my pockets without being a total weirdo about it. Not sure if it works.

"You're not usually out here, are you?" Griffin says. "I don't think I've seen you around."

"Oh, no. Most of the time I take the bus, though my parents do pick me up during soccer. That's where I should be right now. At practice. Except I can't play. And I missed the bus. Which is why my sister's coming to get me."

"Aha," Griffin says, and he leaves it at that.

This is the other reason why I'm slow to make friends. Talking to new people is hard, even when they're nice. It's like, when they're talking, I can barely focus on what they're saying, because I'm busy trying to figure out what I'm supposed to say next. Then it's my turn to talk, and I'm still not sure, so I end up rambling. It's so much easier to make friends on the soccer field. No talking required.

A steady *oontz-oontz* pulses from the headphone that dangles around Griffin's neck, making it painfully obvious that neither one of us is speaking.

Finally, Griffin notices me staring at the headphone.

"You like electronic music?" he asks.

"Yeah, it's cool," I say, although the truth is, I don't really listen to it much. I like all kinds of music okay. Whatever somebody else puts on is usually good with me.

Griffin smiles. It's a smile that says he's ready to go back to listening to his music now.

"Cool," he says. "Well, Will, I hope you feel better really soon."

"Who are you waiting on?" I blurt out, as if he didn't just try to end the conversation.

"What, like, right now?"

"Yeah."

Griffin sighs. "Well, funny story. I'm like you. I thought I had drama club today, because it's Thursday, but I forgot it was canceled this week because Mr. Ibsen is out of town. My mom's coming to get me." Almost to himself, he adds, "If she ever stops working."

There are so many things I could respond to here. The fact that drama club reminds me of his Cowardly Lion performance. The fact that my parents always seem to be working, too.

The fact that he said, *I'm like you.*

With so many possible things to choose, it's like I can't settle on any of them. Thankfully, I'm saved from the embarrassment of saying the wrong thing by the sight of Lexie's car turning into the pickup lane.

"There's my sister," I say.

Griffin nods. "See you later."

I wave, then move to get in the car.

But something stops me. It's like—maybe because she's right in front of me—I can hear Lexie's voice in my head, telling me I need to branch out and make new friends. And there's a little part of me that feels bad about earlier, when I checked to make sure no one saw me talking to Griffin. Maybe I just feel bad leaving him on his own.

"Hey, Griffin? Do you want a ride?"

Griffin looks surprised, but he also looks glad I asked.

"You sure? Your sister won't mind?"

"She'll be cool with it," I say. *Eventually.*

"Sweet. Let me just text my mom," Griffin says.

While he does that, I tap on the passenger-side window of Lexie's car. She drives an old beige piece of junk that she calls "Stewart" for reasons she refuses to explain. When she rolls down the window, she looks confused and annoyed.

"I'm already late for work, Will. What the heck is going on?"

"Can we give Griffin a ride home?"

"Who the heck is Griffin?"

I point over my shoulder, and Lexie cranes her neck to get a look.

"Does he live near us? My manager is seriously ready to fire me as it is, after an earlier incident with a root beer float."

I shrug, then motion Griffin over so he can tell us. He says his address through the window, and almost as soon as Lexie puts it into her phone, she groans.

"I'll never make it to work on time," she says, sounding panicked.

I feel my whole body flooding with embarrassment. I know this is one hundred percent my fault, but if she doesn't give Griffin a ride now, after I told him we could, I'll die.

"Where do you work?" Griffin asks.

"Scoops and Shakes on Main," she says.

"Oh!" he says. "That's right by the game store where I always hang out. I can just ride with you and have my mom pick me up there later."

Lexie chews her bottom lip. She's probably debating in her head whether it's worse to drop off a stranger at some random store, or whether it's worse to tell that stranger no, when he looks so excited for the ride.

"I can go with him," I say, thinking fast. "And ride home with you after work. Then you definitely won't be late."

This offer seems to push the mental math in our favor.

"Fine," Lexie says, and I breathe a sigh of relief as Griffin and I climb into the car. "But you owe me," she adds.

"Put it on my sibling credit card," I say, and she laughs in surprise. I'm not usually a joker—at least not out loud.

I guess today I'm full of surprises.

6

THE CHAOS

When Lexie drops us off in front of Griffin's game store, I have this moment of wondering what the heck I'm doing here. There's a Spider-Man and a She-Ra painted on two large windows on either side of the door, and I imagine they're the defenders of geek culture, sworn to keep out any imposters who have spent their whole lives playing sports, going to church, and doing no geeky things whatsoever. Imposters who have no place inside their fortress.

"So what do you do here, exactly?" I ask.

"Do you play Mirror Realms?"

"Is that the one with the elves and the magic?"

"You don't have to be an elf," Griffin says. "But yeah, lots of magic. It's a multiplayer RPG, and people log in from all over the world."

"I've seen my friend Luca's older brother playing it, but I've never played it myself." What I don't add is that Luca's older brother is a total hermit who doesn't get along with Luca at all. We only saw him playing Mirror Realms once because we tried to sneak into his room to grab his scooter when we thought he was gone. It didn't end well.

"It's the best game," Griffin says. "And they have these dedicated gaming computers here. I'll show you."

Griffin leads me through the door. "Oh, and don't mind the smell," he whispers over his shoulder. "It's from the sandwich shop next door. For some reason the bread smells even stronger in here than it does in there."

"Griffin! What's up, little dude?"

There's a man behind the counter in a Star Wars T-shirt. He's quickly sorting a large stack of comic books into two white boxes, and he doesn't miss a beat even as he looks up to welcome us.

"Hey, Dan," Griffin calls. "I brought a friend."

"I can see that," Dan says, smiling. "No school today?"

"We just got out," Griffin explains.

Dan pulls out his phone and checks the time in disbelief.

"Go figure," he says.

"We're going to get on the computers," Griffin says. "Can you put Will on my account?"

"No problem," Dan says, before turning back to his comic stack.

Seeing my look of confusion, Griffin tells me, "It's three dollars an hour to use the computers here, but I have a monthly tab. My mom won't mind me adding you for a day."

"Oh," I say. "I have allowance money. I can pay."

"Seriously, don't worry about it."

"Okay. Well, thanks."

I make a note of the bathroom as we pass it on the way to the back. I'm relieved that it's a single user, in case I feel sick later. Still, I hope it doesn't come to that. That would be so embarrassing.

Griffin and I sit down at two computers that already have Mirror Realms installed on them.

"The first thing you have to do is build a character," Griffin says. "Do you want to be in the Militia or the Chaos?"

"Hmm," I say. "Which one are you?"

"The Chaos," Griffin says. "They have cooler powers."

"I'm all for cooler powers."

"Okay, then you have to pick your class. Do you want to be a Fighter, a Scholar, or a Healer?"

"A Healer," I say.

"Sweet," Griffin says. "I'm a Fighter, so that will be good balance when we go on quests."

I glow as if he's paid me a compliment. It's the same way I feel whenever a waiter tells me I've made a good choice on the menu.

"Now you get to pick what you look like."

On the screen, a gray person stands like a mannequin without any features. There are buttons to give the mannequin everything from lips to hair to skin tone to eyes. I can choose how tall my character should be. I can choose their body shape.

There are so many options. It's a little overwhelming.

"What does your character look like?" I ask.

Griffin pulls up his character's profile. His Fighter is a towering, fearsome, blue-skinned guy with huge arm muscles and a giant battle-ax to go with them.

"I'd be scared to face him down on the soccer field," I say.

"Right?" Griffin says. "That's a draconian ax. I had to kill a Vampire Dragon to get it."

"Whoa."

I start to pick out traits for my character. I make it a guy, and I guess I want him to be athletic and intimidating, too, even if he's a Healer. But as soon as I select green eyes and the yellow hair option, I'm surprised to see that my character suddenly looks like a fantasy-world version of Henry.

I feel a jolt of fear. I don't want Griffin to think I'm doing that on purpose—like I'm making fun of him or something. Does he know I'm friends with Henry? Does he suspect I heard about him inviting Henry to the dance?

I quickly give my Healer red hair, then add a unibrow and a gruesome-looking scar, just to make it clear he's not based on anyone in particular.

Griffin doesn't seem to notice anything's wrong.

"Okay, last thing," he says. "You have to pick a name. I'm Griffinlord13, even though I've had this character since I was eleven. I just like the number thirteen better."

"Hmm," I say. I think about it for a second, then decide that since this is Mirror Realms, my name should be the opposite of me. As a joke, I try to input "Won't," but the game won't let me use an apostrophe in my name. So I type "Willnot."

"Willnot. Nice. Now you're ready to go," Griffin says.

"Except when you first start, you're level one and have nothing in your inventory. So let me just . . ." He makes a series of lightning-fast clicks on his mouse, and next thing I know I'm getting a ping and a pop-up saying that Griffinlord13 has sent me a message. When I open the message, I see that Griffin has gifted me all kinds of armor and weapons, from an Onyx helmet to a Runed Staff of Healing. "There," he says. "Now you should be able to survive more than the training battles."

And then we're off and questing. Even with the advanced gear, the game is a little complicated for me, and there's no way I'll ever be able to use a mouse and keyboard as fast as Griffin does. I keep dying in skirmishes because I'm pressing the wrong buttons, healing monsters that I'm supposed to be killing.

Griffin doesn't seem to mind too much, though. Every time I die in an explosion of blue magic, he laughs like it's the funniest thing he's ever seen.

"I can see why you chose the Chaos allegiance," he says.

In spite of the learning curve, I find myself getting into it. I had no idea a video game could be like soccer, pulling me out of my thoughts for a minute, getting my heart pumping every time something exciting happens.

Henry's a sports junkie to the core. No interest in video games whatsoever. And my dad always says too much screen time will rot your brain. But this isn't so bad.

If I'm being honest, it's actually pretty fun.

I'm so caught up in the game, I completely miss the fact that someone is saying my name behind me. Griffin finally has to tap me on the shoulder to get my attention, and when I turn around, I see my mom standing there, her arms crossed over her chest, her mouth in a worried line.

"All right there, bud?" she asks. "Is your phone dead or what?"

I slap a hand to my head.

"It's still on silent from school. I totally forgot."

She lets out an exasperated sigh. I can see the moment when she decides not to ground me in front of my new friend.

"Mom, this is Griffin," I say. "He goes to my school."

"Nice to meet you, Griffin," she says. "Do your parents know you're here?"

Griffin nods.

"It's just me and my mom, but yeah, she's going to pick me up after work."

"Where does your mom work?" my mom asks, in the

nosy way she gets whenever Lexie or I bring home a new friend (usually Lexie, let's be real).

"Do you know Goldy's Bakery?" Griffin asks.

"Is that out on Reed Street?"

"Yes, ma'am."

"Someone brought their donuts to the store for our holiday party last year. Really good. I had a hot chocolate donut."

"I'll tell my mom," Griffin says. "She's Goldy."

"Oh, how lovely," Mom says.

I hurry to log out before my mom can subject Griffin to any more of this torture.

"Thanks again for letting me play on your account," I say.

"Hope to see you around the Mirror Realms," Griffin says. Then, softly enough that my mom won't hear, he adds, "I'm basically online all the time."

"Cool," I say. "I'll see you around."

"Y'all have a good day," Dan says as my mom ushers me out of the store, and she swivels to give him a suspicious glance and a tight smile all at once, though he's not really paying attention. Just keeps sorting comics.

"I thought Lexie was taking me home."

"Yeah, you and Lexie made some big plans without me today, huh?" she says. But she doesn't seem that mad anymore. I think I even see the hint of a real smile. "Lexie got invited to go prom dress shopping with some of her friends. Luckily, she remembered to let me know . . ."

"Okay, okay. I'm sorry about the phone."

"I'm glad you made a new friend, Will. Just please text your father and me *before* you decide to spend all afternoon at a game store next time."

"I will. I promise."

Once we're in the car and buckled, she turns to face me.

"So how was it being back today?"

I think of that bug-in-a-jar feeling I had at school. I think of Coach Yosef saying I couldn't even be team manager.

"It was all right," I say.

"Yeah? Did you feel sick at all?"

"Not really." I'm officially not counting when I had to run to the bathroom at lunch. Especially because, to explain that, I'd have to tell her what Luca was saying about my new friend Griffin.

"Not really, huh? Does that mean a little bit sick?"

"It means not really."

"Okay, I hear you. Hopefully that means the prednisone is already making a difference?"

"Yeah."

We're mostly quiet on the way home after that. Though when we pass Reed Street, she says, "We'll have to make a trip to Goldy's sometime. Those hot chocolate donuts really were something else."

7

STAINED GLASS

I have a confession to make, but first, there's some back-story you need to know.

Every year, right after school lets out for the summer, our church has a lock-in for all the middle school kids. A lock-in is basically a sleepover, except not at a house. They do literally lock the doors with all of us inside, but I think the real reason they call it a lock-in instead of a sleepover is because it sounds more exciting.

Plus, everybody tries to stay up all night, or at least as late as they can. Not much sleeping involved.

Last year was my first time getting to go to the lock-in. I'd heard all about it from Lexie, though, and I'd been telling Henry and Yasmin, my best friends at church, about everything to look forward to. Henry's an only child, and Yasmin is the oldest of her three siblings, so they had no idea until they heard it from me.

The number-one thing we were all excited for was this game called sardines. It's like hide-and-seek, but in reverse. Instead of everyone hiding while one person tries to find them, only one person hides while everyone else looks. If you find the hiding person, you don't say anything. You just hide right next to them, like sardines in a tin. Eventually, everyone ends up hiding together, but before that, you get to walk all around the church after dark, exploring the rooms and hidden spaces.

I *think* the sanctuary is supposed to be off limits. But that night last year, when Henry and I were wandering around the church together, trying to find Madison during her turn to hide, the door to the sanctuary wasn't locked. And no one had told us specifically to stay out of there. So we just went in.

You have to understand, the energy at a lock-in is just, like, electric. School's finally out. You're in the church with only a few parents and youth group leaders for supervision. Me personally, I didn't have any Crohn's disease symptoms at that point. I was honestly a little hyper. Not worried about a thing.

Anyway, I tell you all this so you know how Henry and I came to be playing with the little bean bag we always bring to kick around before our soccer games, *inside* the sanctuary. We were passing it back and forth, which we'd never do inside on a normal day. We truly know better.

Oh, and you should know that our sanctuary has a *lot* of stained glass. Like, the ratio of stained-glass window to regular wall space is one to one. There are pictures of crosses and Jesus and the apostles on them. They fill the sanctuary with colorful light on Sundays, and they stretch all the way up to the top of the tall ceiling. It's really something.

So, okay, enough stalling: I was just trying to pass that bean bag back to Henry. I guess I passed it much harder than I meant to. That thing is like a missile if you kick it hard enough.

There was a startling *crack*, and then Henry almost let out a curse word. I'm glad he didn't, since we were in the sanctuary, and that would have made things ten times worse.

Not that things weren't bad already. There were thin, spidery lines in the window behind Henry that hadn't been there before. The glass was clearly broken right near the bottom, in a greenish-blue square that luckily didn't have a person in it. Only color. There wasn't an outright hole in the window, but the cracks were hard to miss.

"What do we do?" I remember asking.

"We? I didn't do this!" Henry protested.

Right then, Yasmin opened the door to the sanctuary. She said, "You guys aren't supposed to be in here," like she'd heard some announcement we'd missed.

I bugged out my eyes at Henry, begging him not to say anything. Much to my relief, he didn't. Not that night, and not in the weeks afterward, when word started spreading around church that one of the stained-glass windows had a new cracks in it, and they were going to have to find a specialist who would know how to fix it.

It took all summer before it was finally fixed. When it was done, Dr. Gregory, our pastor, even made an announcement in front of the whole church, about how our church had finally healed, and Yasmin shot me this look across the room, like somehow she'd figured out that I was the one who broke it.

Even though the window is almost as good as new now, with a windowpane that's only a *little* bluer than the panes around it, I still sometimes feel sick about it, nearly a year later. I don't know if Henry even thinks about it anymore. If he does, he never says.

But me?

I'm just waiting for the day when Dr. Gregory or Mr. Dyson or someone else in the church calls me into their office, to tell me they *know*.

That breaking the window was bad enough, but not telling anyone I did it made it even worse.

Today, at Weekend Warriors, Mr. Dyson is leading a discussion about the book of First Corinthians. While the rest of us sit in a semicircle around our table, Mr. Dyson leans against the whiteboard at the front of the classroom. He opens his Bible, which has so many little bookmarks sticking out of it that I have no idea how he remembers which one he actually needs. He reads a passage that says, "Bad company corrupts good morals," and then asks the class, "What do you think Paul meant by that?"

Madison is the first person to answer, which is often the case. Madison's dad is a deacon at the church, and I think they must have extra Bible study at home, because she already seems to know all the passages we're supposed to be learning in class.

"It means that if you hang out with bad people, they will make you bad, too."

"Thank you, Madison," Mr. Dyson says. "Anyone else?"

There are ten of us total in Weekend Warriors. Me, Henry, Yasmin, Madison, and Zander are all seventh graders, although I don't see Yasmin and Zander outside of church, since Yasmin goes to private school and Zander is homeschooled. Then there are two eighth graders and three sixth graders, and while they *do* all go to Oakwood with me, the grades don't mix much at school unless you're on a team or a club together, so Weekend Warriors is the only place I really see them, too.

Mr. Dyson wants us to be this tight-knit group, though. That's why, as a class, we did all kinds of trust exercises at the beginning of the year. One person would have to close their eyes and fall backward while everyone else caught them. The idea was to show that anything you said in class would stay in class. That this class was a safe space to try out new thoughts, and no answer was out of bounds if it was from the heart.

I ended up hitting the ground during that exercise,

because Henry thought it would be funny if they dropped me a little bit, and it turns out it's hard not to drop someone all the way once you start.

I probably deserved that, in payback for the window. And they broke my fall enough that it didn't hurt.

It wouldn't have mattered if they'd caught me anyway. Ten people still feels like a lot of people for a safe space. I hardly ever speak up in class.

"Will? What do you think?" Mr. Dyson asks.

"I agree with Madison," I say.

Mr. Dyson gives me a sad smile. Just like all the rest of my teachers this week, he's been looking at me like Crohn's disease is fatal, and I'm very brave just for existing. It's nice to know all these people care about me, but I think I'm ready for the grace period of niceness to be over. If I have to suffer through everybody's attention, I'd rather it be for something good, like winning the championship tournament.

"Thanks, Will," Mr. Dyson says. "What I wonder is, how do we know which company is bad? Y'all know we've said in this class before that there are no bad people, only bad actions. And Jesus says to forgive your neighbor and love your enemies. So how do we square those teachings with this reminder from Paul?"

To my surprise, it's Henry who speaks up. Henry is in his element when he's cutting up and making jokes, but he knows there's a time and place for everything. Whenever we have a more serious class discussion, he usually stays quiet, like me.

"I think it's saying that people who don't believe in Jesus and follow His word—their beliefs can rub off on you. So you can forgive them and feel bad for them and stuff, but you have to watch what you learn from them."

"Very well said, Henry," Mr. Dyson says, now with a genuine smile. "Did the rest of you catch what Henry just said? Henry, why don't you say that again just to give everyone a chance to let it resonate."

So Henry repeats his reading, all but glowing from the praise.

I didn't tell Henry about going to the game store with Griffin on Thursday. I almost did at lunch on Friday. I had a whole speech prepared in my head. *The funniest thing happened after I left y'all at soccer practice*, I was going to say. *You know that game Luca's brother plays? Turns out it's actually cool.*

But almost as soon as we sat down, Luca said to Henry,

"Any more guys ask you to the dance today?" and Henry said, "Shut up, Luca," with this angry, un-Henry-like look on his face. It sounded like things had gotten tense at soccer practice after I left, because people weren't playing very well in the scrimmage, and Coach said they weren't taking the tournament seriously. I decided I'd better not poke the hornet's nest.

"All right, Warriors," Mr. Dyson says. "That's our time for today. Go forth and be awesome."

That's how Mr. Dyson ends every class, and I used to like it. But this year it's been harder to make myself feel awesome. Not just because of the Crohn's disease, either.

This year, I've started to feel like Weekend Warriors might be one more T-E-A-M where there are no *I*'s allowed. Like when Mr. Dyson and Madison—and even Henry, I guess—talk about "bad company," what they mean is people like Francis Redmond and Griffin Miller, who wear rainbow socks and ask other boys to the dance.

People who don't really fit in on teams and in tight-knit groups.

At least not around here.

I never really got a chance to know Francis Redmond, but I spent a day with Griffin, and he seemed like good company to me.

So why is it so hard to tell Henry that?

8

CHICKEN AND DUMPLINGS

In the game of Mirror Realms, there are lots of areas on the map you can visit. These are the "realms" from the name of the game. So far, I've been to the water realm, the desert realm, the grass realm, and the dream realm.

The dream realm is my favorite because you can't get into any fights there, but you can still level up by cultivating dream magic from the dream caches. Griffin says it's normal to have to cultivate a lot of dream magic before you're ready for battle.

I've settled into a routine over the past couple days. When I get home from school, I go straight to the computer in the den and commence the cultivating. I've already gotten my Healer all the way up to level nine that way.

Griffin logs in a little later, and then we head out into the fighting realms together, on quests to try to get high-level loot. I'm not accidentally healing the monsters anymore, but I'm still not much of an asset in a battle. If Griffin were as competitive at this game as Luca is at soccer, he would've ditched me after the first day.

I can tell Mom and Dad don't love the fact that I'm using my time off from soccer to play a video game. Last night, when they came home from work and found me glued to the computer, they made a new house rule on the spot that I can't play Mirror Realms after dinner. They're lucky we can't download games on our school laptops, or I might be tempted to sneak in a few more dream caches in my room.

No one is more skeptical about Mirror Realms than Lexie, though. She walked by when I was in the middle of a quest, mouse-clicking up a storm, and said, "Who is this nerd and what has he done with my brother?" Pretty rich considering she's the one who said I needed to branch out and make other friends. Anyway, my parents shot death lasers at her with their eyes, and later I overheard Mom in Lexie's room saying that they all needed to be kinder about the ways I was "filling my time" while I'm still not feeling well.

Because . . . yeah. It's been a whole week since I started taking prednisone, and I still felt winded just trying to help bring in the groceries from the car today. I still have to leave some of my classes as soon as the bell rings to go to the bathroom. My stomach still hurts if I eat the wrong foods.

Just so we're clear, I'm pretty sure the list of wrong foods is longer than the list of foods that are okay. Dr. Clarkson says this is another thing that's only true during a flare-up, which is what they call it when all your symptoms are going haywire. When I'm back in remission, and the symptoms are under control, she swears I'll be able to eat popcorn, chicken wings, and ice cream again. Until then, the list of dangerous foods she sent home with me last week includes anything spicy or greasy, dairy of all kinds, caffeinated drinks, and on and on.

It even includes "roughage," which is a fancy word for fruits, vegetables, and beans. Just in case you were thinking it was only unhealthy foods I'm supposed to avoid.

At dinner tonight, I look up from my chicken and dumplings, which Mom made without celery because apparently that's roughage in the extreme, and I see my dad staring at me across the table. When I catch him, he tries to act like he was in the process of looking all around the room.

"How's it going with the salt intake, bud?" he finally says.

"All right," I say, although the fact that he's asking makes me think that it might not be going all right after all. Dr. Clarkson said I needed to limit how much salt I eat while I'm on prednisone because the medicine makes me hold more water than a well, and limiting salt is supposed to help me avoid "moon face," which is a common side effect.

(Whoever came up with that phrase—moon face—I'd like to have a word with them. I mean, come on.)

I've been checking my face in the mirror every day, and I don't *think* I look different . . . at least not yet. But it's hard to track changes when you're basing them off the mirror, because changes can be so gradual, you don't even notice. It's not until you look at an old picture or something that you realize how far you've come. Like, when I had my growth spurt last year, I was as surprised as anybody when I did my physical with Dr. Yi and discovered I'd gotten a whole seven inches taller since my previous physical.

"Have you been doing push-ups or anything this week?" Dad continues.

I shake my head.

"Now that you don't have soccer, maybe you should think of another way to get some light physical activity in. What if we played a round of tennis on Saturday? We can just lob it, no serving, so you don't have to do any running."

"Yeah, maybe," I say.

"Hmm," Dad says.

Here's the thing. I will lob a tennis ball with my dad if it will make him happy. But from where I'm sitting, if I'm well enough to play tennis, I should be well enough to play soccer. I'm not playing soccer because I still feel bad. "Light physical activity" is kind of an oxymoron.

I think Mom's mind must've gone to soccer, too. "So, round one of the tournament is tomorrow, huh?" she says. "You still planning to go watch?"

"Of course. Why wouldn't I?" I say, a little defensively.

"Just making sure Lexie is still supposed to come get you after she's done at work," Mom says. Now that I'm not playing in the game, she and Dad figure it's not worth taking time off work themselves to come watch.

Lexie looks up from her phone and flashes me a very sarcastic smile.

"You're welcome," she says.

"Thank you," I say.

I'm actually pretty nervous for tomorrow's game, and it has nothing to do with Gordon Middle School's team. (I hate to sound mean, but they're not very good.)

After the game ends, Henry has a big surprise planned to (finally) invite Julie to the spring dance, and I got roped into it because I'm going to be in the bleachers anyway. I can't miss the game even if I wanted to. And the thing is, I *do* sort of want to miss it now. The attention might be mostly on Henry and Julie, but I can't help feeling like there'll be a big spotlight on me too, right when I most wish I could disappear on the sidelines.

What if I get sick at the exact moment Henry needs me?

What if I have to run to the bathroom while everybody is watching?

"Is your new computer friend going to be there?" Dad says. "What's his name . . . Grayson?"

"Griffin," I say. "No, he's not going to be there."

"He doesn't like soccer?" Dad asks, as if not liking

soccer is a terrible crime.

"I don't know," I say. "He's just going to be busy."

I know this, because when I told Griffin I couldn't be on Mirror Realms tomorrow—which I'm actually kind of bummed about, because we were *this* close to earning the Magma sword today, after getting the Volcano Knight down to his last five hit points on two separate runs— Griffin just said, *No worries, me neither.* I'd forgotten that since tomorrow is Thursday, he'll have drama club. He didn't even ask me where I'd be.

Honestly, I was kind of relieved he didn't. Drama club or no, I don't think Griffin would want to be at the soccer game if he knew he'd have to watch Henry invite Julie to the dance when it's over. But I can't exactly warn him. He still doesn't know that I know he asked Henry, and plus Henry's big invitation is supposed to be a surprise.

I don't know how I became a person who has all these secrets. I didn't do it on purpose—that's for sure.

"Can I have some more chicken and dumplings?" I ask.

"You sure about that, bud?" Dad asks.

"I went light on the salt," Mom tells him.

"Well, then," Dad says, "I guess that's okay . . ."

I get another helping of chicken and dumplings, but

74

only a small one. Then I push it around in my bowl, only taking a couple bites. It doesn't taste as good as it normally does. I don't think it has anything to do with the lack of salt.

9

NAIL-BITER

I make my way down to the soccer field, self-conscious about the fact that I'm coming straight from seventh period and not from the locker room with the rest of the team. A lot of parents are already in the bleachers or on folding chairs they brought from home, but I'm one of the first students to arrive.

All according to plan.

I scope out a spot on the front row of the bleachers and quickly hide my bookbag under my seat. The poster board Henry handed me at lunch is rolled up and poking out of the top, and the bags of confetti are bulging out of the little pocket.

I don't know about your school, but at Oakwood, spring

dance invitations are out of control. It all started a few years ago, when this guy Carl Mazzio at Oakwood had an older brother whose high school "promposal" went viral on social media. I've seen the video, and I thought it was whatever—basically, this girl walks out of her front door and finds her name spelled out in all these flowers—but I guess fifty thousand people disagreed.

Anyway, Carl Mazzio got the idea that a flower invitation could land him a date, too. And I guess fifty thousand people know better than I do, because it worked *again*. That was enough to make over-the-top invitations go viral at Oakwood.

I remember hearing about it all when Lexie was in middle school and got invited by a boy named Blake, with help from an honest-to-goodness Rube Goldberg machine in their science class. (When she told our family the story, I was way more interested in the machine than the dance.) But seeing the invitations in action last year was on a whole other level.

This year, now that we're in seventh grade and expected to go to the *real* spring dance, it feels like there's all this pressure on my grade to live up to the hype.

Exhibit A: the poster board and confetti currently

hiding in my bookbag.

The bleachers are starting to fill up, so I set my jacket on the space beside me, reserving the seat. Already the butterflies in my stomach are getting intense, so I take a few steadying breaths before those butterflies become full-on stomach pains.

I can mostly see the parking lot from here. Well enough to see the Gordon Middle School bus pull up and let off a team of guys who look more like they're piling out of a clown car than gearing up for the championship tournament.

We played them once already in the regular season, and what I remember from that game is how they didn't take it seriously. Coach Yosef always tells us to have fun and keep things in perspective, but for them, it was something different. Like they were so sure they were going to lose, they wanted to laugh at themselves before we could laugh at them. Judging from all that goofing off by the bus, I'd say they're ready to do the same today.

I feel a jolt of jealousy when the Oakwood locker room doors burst open and the team—*my* team—comes running out, all pumped up and ready to go. They take the field in a whirlwind of energy, running drills and dribbling balls while the Gordon guys make the walk from the visitors' entrance. Henry scans the crowd, spots me, and gives me a thumbs-up with a question mark in his eyes. I return the thumbs-up and move my feet a little so he can see the bookbag. He smiles and does a fist pump before joining the other guys to warm up.

Finally, about five minutes before the game is supposed to start, I spot Julie walking up to the bleachers with her friend Ashley. Ashley plays on the girls' soccer team, and her being here is *not* according to plan, but luckily the space I reserved with my jacket should be big enough for two.

"Julie! Ashley!" I call out to them. "Over here!"

"Oh! Hey, Will!" Julie says, smiling but a little surprised that I'm calling her name. Julie's in fifth-period history with me, but we don't really know each other that well. I think she's just nice to everyone. "Is that seat saved?"

"Yes, for you," I say, then immediately realize my mistake. If I'm not careful, I could ruin Henry's surprise. "I mean, it wasn't before, but you two can sit here if you want."

"So . . . you're not waiting on someone? Or you are?" Julie says, now totally confused. Then she breaks into a smile. "Like Griffin?"

"Uh, what?" I say, and I'm pretty sure I start blushing.

"He told me he's got you playing Mirror Realms," she explains. And then, when *I'm* the one who looks confused, she adds, "I go on quests with him sometimes. I'm a Scholar."

"Oh," I say, my heartbeat slowing and my smile picking up. "Cool. I had no idea."

"Yeah. We go way back. I'm nowhere near as good as he is, but it's fun."

"She tried to get me to play too," Ashley says as they sit down. "*So* not for me. When it comes to video games, give me Mario Party or a dance game any day."

The ref's whistle draws our attention back to the field, and just like that, the first round of the championship tournament is underway.

I didn't know how much I was going to miss being out there until right this moment.

I'm not proud to admit it, but I'm a little bummed to see just how good Amit is at center midfield. He runs super fast and passes with laser precision. Maybe Henry was only being nice when he said Amit's not as good as me, or maybe Amit is one of those guys who really ramps it up in an actual game, but in every play where he gets the ball, I find myself doing a comparison and coming up short. One of my favorite things about playing center midfield has always been that I'm not the one scoring and I'm not the one at goal. It's a key support role, but it's not a star-maker. At least, I didn't think so. Amit's making me rethink that assessment.

Henry's playing well at striker, too. He is *definitely* one of those guys who plays better in games when the stakes are real.

It's funny, though. For as good as our guys are playing, the Gordon players aren't the pushovers I expected them to be.

Just before the end of the first quarter, Henry makes a power shot that I'm sure is going to be a goal, but the Gordon goalie manages to block it by diving and tipping the ball off with his fingers. It's an incredible save, I've got to admit. I've seen Luca make a couple like that in practice, but not many, and never in a high-stakes tournament game.

The Gordon guys are still cutting up and having fun

like they did in the regular season, but this time, instead of making them sloppy, it's making them work more like a team.

At halftime, the game is still tied at 0–0. I wish I could hear the pep talk Coach Yosef gives the Acorns. Everybody's sweating through their jerseys and dumping their water bottles over their heads, even though it's cold enough that I had to put my jacket back on.

The guys get back out there for the second half, and whatever Coach said, it seems to be working. Right away, our forwards have the ball deep in Gordon territory, and it's like Henry has a magnet on his shoes—the Gordon guys just can't get the ball away from him.

All the Acorn fans start shouting and standing up. It's one of those moments where you can feel the momentum. Players from both teams are jamming around the Gordon goal. If one of our guys could get just one opening—

Bam!

Henry takes a shot from the outside at full speed, and the ball flies like a comet, straight into the top-right corner of the goal. No dive in the world could have blocked that shot.

Everybody cheers.

Julie and Ashley and I give one another high fives, shouting in disbelief. That shot from Henry was one in a hundred.

But the goal only fires up the Gordon guys more. The second they get possession, they put on an offensive clinic, running circles around our defense and charging Luca at goal. Luca stands ready, and when the Gordon guys take a shot, he makes a valiant jump and a block, but the Gordon striker is right there to catch the rebound, and he lands a shot to a wide-open goal before Luca can get back on his feet.

Groans of disappointment echo through the crowd, but no one looks more upset than Luca, who smacks his hands on his knees and shouts what I'm pretty sure is, "Where was my defense?"

He's not wrong, but it's so like Luca to want to find blame somewhere else. I know he's just mad because the Gordon game was supposed to be a cakewalk.

Heading into the fourth quarter, the game is still tied at 1–1, and you can feel the nerves in the air. The tournament is double elimination, but once you get that first loss, you have a much longer bracket to climb if you want to make it to the finals, and that means less time off in between games. Everybody knows that rested teams are the ones that win when it counts.

Players swap in and out on both sides, but the reserve players come in stiff and jittery, while the guys who've been playing the whole game are looking really tired.

The game alone is stressful enough.

But for me, it's really starting to sink in that at the end of this quarter, Henry is supposed to run over here, and I'm supposed to help him ask Julie to the dance.

Yes, I had thought about the distant possibility that Henry could be coming over here after a *losing* game, and I'm sure Henry thought of that, too, even playing against Gordon. Somehow, though, I don't think either of us imagined that the game would be such a nail-biter.

If this game comes down to the wire, is Henry really going to be ready to switch gears and go through with this invitation?

If the team loses at the last second, will the other guys forgive him for hogging the spotlight and making their moment of defeat about the spring dance? Is that sportsmanlike?

Coach will probably be furious.

Maybe he'll even be mad at me for being part of it. Maybe he won't let me have my spot back.

That's when I feel it.

That sinking, heavy feeling in my stomach that lets me know I need to get to a bathroom. That I'm about to be sick.

Oh no.

I close my eyes for a second and take a deep breath, trying to make the feeling go away.

But it only gets worse.

If I don't get to a bathroom ASAP, I'm going to have a humiliating accident right here on the sidelines, and it will be a million times worse than having everybody look at me because of some silly dance invitation.

"Uh, Julie, could you save my seat?" I say quickly. "I have to run to the restroom."

"Oh, uh—sure, okay," Julie says, hardly taking her eyes off the field. I can hear the note of surprise in her voice. Who in their right mind would leave the game at its most exciting, decisive moment?

But I don't have time to care about that now.

I stand up and move as quickly as I can without outright sprinting. I don't want to draw too much attention to myself, and anyway, I don't think I could run if I wanted to. It's taking my full concentration to keep my stomach in check.

I head toward the bathroom all the way back in the English hall. There's a closer one in the fieldhouse where the vending machines are, but that bathroom is notoriously disgusting, with just one dingy stall that has a broken lock. It usually doesn't even have toilet paper in it.

So back to the school it is.

It's weird that I find myself praying during this moment, but that's what happens all the same. I pray that I will make it to the bathroom before I have an accident, and I pray that I won't run into anyone I know on the way. I tell myself that if God will just answer these two specific prayers, I'll be so much better from here on out. I'll do whatever Mr. Dyson says I should do. I'll even pay more attention during Dr. Gregory's sermons.

Thankfully, my prayers are answered this time.

I'll spare you the full details of what it's like going to the bathroom when you have Crohn's disease.

It's hard to talk about, to be honest. There are so many different ways it can be gross and scary, and the grossness of it all makes me feel like *I'm* gross, too.

For now, I'll tell you this: going to the bathroom with Crohn's disease can take a long time, because sometimes your stomach hurts in a way that makes you *think* you still have to go when you really don't. But just as often, you really do still have to go.

And if you're not sure which it is, better safe than sorry.

By the time I make it back to the top of the stairs overlooking the soccer field, I can see right away that the game is over.

Players on both sides are still putting on their sweatpants and hoodies, but most of the guys on our team have joined their parents on the sidelines. Even the line of postgame high fives is already done.

There are too many people crowded around the bleachers to spot Julie, Ashley, or Henry from here. I'll have to get closer.

But there is one bright spot: it's obvious from everyone's energy alone that we did it.

We won.

The Gordon guys look absolutely crushed. All the joking around from earlier is gone. I kind of feel bad for them—they really did play well—but I also feel like, at least they got to play.

I hustle as much as I can down the stairs, then push my way through the crowd. I give Luca a quick thumbs-up as I pass, though he hardly notices me because he's deep in conversation with his parents, and all three of them still look tense from the game. That's for the best: I have to get to my bookbag before Julie leaves and I ruin Henry's invitation.

But when I make it to where I was sitting with Julie and Ashley, Julie is already holding the posterboard. The one that says *Will You Go to the Dance with Me?* in green marker, in handwriting that is only forgivable because it belongs to Henry. There's confetti all over the ground at her feet. My bookbag is propped up against the front row of the bleachers.

"Will!" I hear, as Henry throws his arm around my shoulder. "We did it! We're through round one!"

"I saw!" I say, trying hard to match his enthusiasm.

I raise an eyebrow in Julie's direction. My brain is starting to catch up with my eyes, but it's not all the way there yet.

"She said yes!" Henry shouts, which finally draws Julie's attention. She turns to us with the biggest smile on her face.

"Will, you were so sweet to help Henry with his invitation," she says.

"I was?"

"Totally," Henry says. "What would I have done if you hadn't snuck in the poster and the confetti?"

I am so relieved.

It's probably the win that is making them nicer than they have to be. Whatever it is, I'll take it.

Henry leans in close when Julie and Ashley go back to talking.

"You feeling okay?" he asks.

I rotate my hand at the wrist: *So-so.*

He nods.

I feel a tap on my shoulder, and when I turn, Amit is there, with a stone-faced expression and two adults behind him I recognize from the sidelines. They were cheering the whole game. Now, they look as happy as Amit looks serious.

"Hi, Will," Amit says. "These are my parents."

"Nice to meet you," I say, returning their smiles. I wonder if they know I'm the guy whose position Amit played today. Maybe they're about to ask me if I saw how good their son was out there.

Amit takes a deep breath. "We just wanted to tell you that we hope you get better soon."

"Yes," his father says. "You and Amit should be taking turns next week. It's too much playing time for one person."

"Oh," I reply, now feeling like a royal jerk. "Thank you, sir."

He nods, then Amit's family turns to head out.

"Hey, Amit?" I say, stopping him. "You were really good out there today. Like—really, really good."

Amit breaks into a grin.

"Yeah?" he asks.

"Yeah."

"Thanks, Will. That means a lot."

And the funny thing is, it means a lot that it means

a lot. I don't know—maybe that sounds stupid. It's not like I know Amit that well.

But after not feeling like part of the team's opening round win, and not feeling like part of Henry's invitation, I'm glad to feel like part of *something* today—like there's a special club that only center midfielders can join.

And it's nice to know that, when I do get better, there'll be even more of a team waiting to take me back.

10

BALLOONS AND RAINBOWS

Dr. Clarkson's main office isn't the same place where I had my colonoscopy. That procedure was in a massive hospital right in the center of Atlanta. Her main office is a squat, square building on a stretch of road with a bunch of other doctors' offices, like they all got together when they were buying real estate. It's about an hour and a half from our house.

My dad took the day off work to bring me up here. We mostly listened to music on the drive. He likes country, and even though I don't really listen to it when I'm on my own, I like it okay when it's Dad and me together.

Just once, he turned down the volume to say that he wanted to make sure we told Dr. Clarkson about what happened at the game yesterday.

"It wasn't a big deal," I said. "Just a case of bad timing."

"You've been on that steroid for over a week already," Dad said. "And Dr. Clarkson said it should kick in after a few days. I just want to make sure it's working right."

Today was supposed to be a follow-up visit to go over the biopsy results and have an in-person check-in. It wasn't supposed to be the day when I told Dr. Clarkson things were getting worse. I was hoping she would clear me to play soccer again at this visit, but I don't think that'll happen if I tell her the steroid's not working.

I'm one of only two patients in Dr. Clarkson's waiting room. The other patient is a boy way younger than me, here with a woman who looks like she's probably his mom. I'd guess he's about six or seven. I hate that a kid that young might be going through what I'm going through. I at least had a few normal school years, so I know what I'm missing. He probably hasn't even had a chance to join a sports team yet.

"Will?"

A nurse reads my name off her clipboard. She's standing in the doorway that leads back to the patient rooms. When I get up, the other boy watches me carefully, the worry clear on his face.

I give him a small smile, even though I'm not in the best mood myself, to let him know that everything will be okay when they call his name. I really hope it is.

The nurse leads us to a patient room that's dominated by brightly colored balloons and rainbows crisscrossing on the wallpaper. They remind me of Dr. Yi's stickers—something to make little kids like the boy in the waiting room forget they're at a doctor's office. For me, though, they only make it more obvious that's where I am—a helpless little kid who can't even control when he has to go to the bathroom.

In a minute there's a knock on the door, and Dr. Clarkson comes in, followed by a guy in a white doctor's coat. The guy has circular glasses that make his eyes look huge. He doesn't seem old enough to be a doctor. He barely looks older than Lexie.

"Hello, Will," Dr. Clarkson says. "How are we doing today?"

I've started to notice that Dr. Clarkson says "we" a lot. I'm not sure if by "we" she just means me, or if she means me and my dad, or if she means all four of us in the room. I look to my dad in case he plans to answer, but when he gives me an encouraging nod, I say, "Doing all right."

Dad does one of those fake throat-clearing things, as if he wants me to elaborate. I widen my eyes at him to let him know that I'll get to the bad stuff in a minute. I just don't want to start there. Especially not with a stranger in the room.

As if she can tell what I'm thinking, Dr. Clarkson motions to the guy behind her. "This is one of my residents, Dr. Lee. *Resident* means he's still a student doctor, and he's learning here so he can help people like you on his own one day. Is it okay if Dr. Lee asks you some questions to get us started?"

"Oh, um—sure," I say, wondering if anyone has ever answered *no* to that question.

"Great," Dr. Clarkson says. "I'll be back in just a moment."

I didn't realize she was going to be gone when I agreed to this. I feel like she just pulled an epic fake-out on me.

Dr. Lee smiles really big and says, "Hey there, Will. I hear you're a soccer player."

"Yeah," I say. "Usually."

"That's awesome," Dr. Lee says. "I used to play soccer myself when I was your age."

"Oh, cool," I say, relaxing a little bit. "What position?"

"Defense," Dr. Lee says, "although I wasn't very good. I'm sure you're much better at it than I was."

I don't really know what to say to that, so I just sort of smile.

"So, Will, how many times have you been going to the bathroom each day?"

"I . . . um . . ."

"Just on average. It can be a range if that's easier."

"Five or six?" I say, like it's a question.

"And what are they like?" he asks, as breezily as if we're still talking about what soccer position we play.

I feel like I'm hovering somewhere outside my body. The exam room suddenly seems much smaller and warmer. I can feel the heat rising up my neck and onto my cheeks. My dad tries to hide his own discomfort, but he's never been very good at masking his emotions. He's more of a numbers guy.

I do my best to answer Dr. Lee's question, and the next one, and the next one, even though each one feels more embarrassing than the one before. I don't even want to tell you what the questions are—that's how embarrassing they are. They're so personal, and I just met this guy.

"You're doing a great job, bud," Dr. Lee finally says. "Just one more question and then I'll go fetch Dr. Clarkson. How's your mood? Any unexpected mood swings in the last week?"

I know he's asking because of the prednisone. I swear I even notice his eyes darting to my cheeks as he asks, looking for signs of moon face.

I shake my head no, my embarrassment complete.

I've never had a guy doctor before, even if he's just a resident. To be honest, I don't think I like it very much. It's too easy to picture him going out into the hall and laughing about everything I just told him. That's what he'd do if he was one of the guys at school.

Griffin isn't like that, at least. He doesn't try to use what you say to make fun of you. So I guess it's not all guys. But most guys, for sure.

"All right. That's it from me, Will. Dr. Clarkson will be in with you shortly. I hope you feel better very soon."

"Thanks," I mumble.

As soon as he closes the door behind him, Dad and I both let out these gigantic breaths.

"Gosh," Dad says.

"Yeah," I say.

"You're a tough kid," Dad says. "You know that?"

When Dr. Clarkson comes back, one of the first things she does is pull up the pictures from my colonoscopy on her computer.

I knew they were taking pictures at the time, but still. It's incredibly weird to see the inside of your intestines. They don't really look like anything else. I guess I'm glad if this will help me feel better, but I can't help wondering if this is something humans were meant to be able to do, or if it's like one of those horror movies, where the scientists go too far.

"Do you see these little rough red spots?" Dr. Clarkson says. "That's the inflammation. And the biopsy results are consistent with that. But the good news is, it's all moderate inflammation. It's not severe yet. A couple spots we'll keep an eye on, but nothing our current medication plan shouldn't be able to treat."

"We actually have a little concern we were going to ask you about," Dad says. "You want to tell Dr. Clarkson about yesterday, bud?"

I give him a look that could boil water. Did he have to call it a *concern*? Now it's going to be a much bigger deal than it needed to be. I'm starting to regret telling him anything at all.

"Or I could tell her?" Dad says.

"What happened yesterday?" Dr. Clarkson asks.

I let out a big sigh. I say, "Nothing major. I was just at a soccer game, and I had to leave my seat to go to the bathroom."

"And remember," Dad says, apparently determined to ruin my day, "you told your mom and me that it was pretty painful?"

"I guess so," I say. "I mean, it's been like that before. But yeah."

Dr. Clarkson gives me a sympathetic smile.

"That'll happen with Crohn's disease, I'm afraid. How did your stomach feel after you went to the bathroom? Any better?"

"A little," I say.

"And have you noticed any improvement in general this week?"

The truth is, it's kind of hard to say. It's like tracking changes in the mirror. One day I'll feel better, and the next I'll feel worse. My energy level's still not great, but I think my stomach pains aren't as bad? It all evens out.

"A little," I repeat. "I mean, I think so."

"Hmm," she says. "Well, improvement is good. That's what we want to hear. But I don't want to give it too long if the prednisone isn't working."

"What happens then?" Dad asks.

"There are other medicines we can try, but they have more serious side effects, so we try not to use them as a first resort."

More serious than moon face and mood swings? I almost ask. *And what happens if those don't work, either?*

But there are some questions it's better not to ask. That's what people like Coach Yosef mean when they talk about the power of positive thinking, right? If you dwell on the bad stuff, it will make the bad stuff come true.

"How long until I can play soccer again?" I ask. Our next game is coming up, against Pine Mills, and while I'm not as worried about letting the team down now that I've seen Amit in action, I still want to be well enough to play. Pine Mills had a bye in round one because they're the top seed after the regular season. They crushed us in round two of the tournament last year. Oakwood is going to need all the help we can get.

"That all depends on how you're feeling," Dr. Clarkson says.

That's the last thing I want to hear. It's like I'm right back where I started, when it felt like my fault that I couldn't keep up at practice. Can't these high-tech biopsies and photos tell them everything they need to know? I don't *know* how I'm feeling. At least not compared to how I *should* be feeling. That's the whole problem.

Dad says, "I think maybe you'd better not travel to any of the away games, bud, until you're doing a little better. We wouldn't want you to have an accident."

"That's probably a good idea," Dr. Clarkson says. "I know it's no fun in the short term, but just in these first few weeks while you're finding your new normal, it's probably better to avoid stepping out of your comfort zone too much. No strenuous activity, no straying too far from a bathroom, that sort of thing."

I can feel my ears burning. If I squeeze my hands together any harder, I might break a knuckle.

Last week, Dr. Clarkson said, *Any amount of time feeling bad is too long to feel bad.* Now she's saying I need to give it a few weeks to find a "new normal."

"It really wasn't that bad yesterday," I say, and I hate that it comes out sounding like a whine.

Even if it *was* that bad yesterday—even if it scared me a little, too—why is the solution to make me give up more? Why isn't the solution to make me better faster?

"Well," Dad says, "I'm glad you're feeling better about yesterday. But the point is to make sure it's not worse the next time."

We wouldn't want you to have an accident.

An "accident." Like I'm still in kindergarten, instead of twelve years old. And just like a kindergartner, I have this sudden urge to throw a temper tantrum. To tear down this rainbow-and-balloon wallpaper so it will stop mocking me. Making me feel small.

But I don't throw a temper tantrum, as much as I want to.

I keep it all inside, like a big kid is supposed to do.

When the appointment is over, I can't get back to the parking lot fast enough.

Dad and I listen to country music the whole way home.

11

DANCE LESSONS

The next day, Dad decides it's finally time to clean out and completely rearrange the garage—a chore he's been talking about and putting off doing for months.

"I don't know what came over him," Mom says, bringing me a plate of pancakes, drowning in syrup, just the way I like them. Thank goodness pancakes are still on the list of foods I can eat. "He just woke up and got straight to work."

I have a theory. My guess is this is Dad's way of getting out of the tennis game he suggested on Wednesday. I think he'd rather avoid me than admit that tennis might be a "strenuous activity" after all, based on what Dr. Clarkson said yesterday.

Whatever.

Not like I wanted to play tennis anyway.

I'm all too happy to log into Mirror Realms instead. My original plan is to cultivate some more dream magic, but there's an announcement on the login screen that any precious gems found today will be doubled in your inventory, so I decide a trip to the crystal realm is in order. The only problem is, the crystal realm is a fighting realm, and I still keep dying during low-level encounters. Even a team of three crystal crabs forces a respawn, and that should be an easy fight by now.

Around eleven o'clock, I get a ping that sounds like a trumpet—*dunh, dun-nuh-nuh!*—letting me know that Griffin has logged in. I know it's Griffin, because he's still the only other player on my friends list.

I send him a direct message.

Finally! I type.

He responds with three question marks. *???*

I keep dying in crystal realm. Need ur help! I say.

Oh haha, he responds. *I thought maybe you were dying to talk to me.*

I stare at his message for a minute. What does he mean? Is the wordplay just his way of being funny? I can't think of anything specific we have to talk about.

When I don't respond right away, he adds, *Julie told me she sat next to you at the soccer game. I think she might be getting on later today. We should all go on a quest together!*

Cool, I type, only because it would probably be weird to type, *What ELSE did Julie tell you?!*

He knows I was at the game.

Does he also know I had to run to the bathroom and miss the winning goal? Does he know Henry asked Julie to the dance and she said yes?

This whole week, Griffin and I have been living in a Mirror Realms fantasy world, in more ways than one. We still haven't talked about how he asked Henry to the dance. We haven't talked about Oakwood stuff at all, really. It's like, when we play this game, real life at Oakwood doesn't exist.

And I guess I was liking it better that way? This sudden reality check feels like a return to Earth, crash-landing style.

Random question, he types. *What do you think about the spring dance?*

I can feel my heartbeat go from zero to sixty. *Mayday. Mayday.*

Is he asking because he *did* hear about Henry and Julie? Or is he asking because . . . because he's planning to ask me?

What if he *does* ask me?

I don't even know.

Idek, I type. The truth: a classic stall tactic. *What about u?*

I'm VERY excited, he types. *I love to dance. I've been taking waltz and tango lessons at this theater in Atlanta where I do acting classes sometimes. I'm going to try out for their summer musical. Should make up for being the stage manager in the drama club play this year.*

Aha, I type.

I'm not sure what else to say. Maybe I should ask him what a stage manager is? But I'm so hung up on the whole dance business. I don't want to yuck Griffin's yum, but he can't possibly think anyone is going to waltz or tango at the spring dance, can he? Even if he doesn't have a Lexie in his life to tell him how things usually go, he's been at Oakwood long enough that he should know what would happen. What everybody would say.

Just thinking about it now has my stomach twisting in painful knots. I can see it all so clearly in my head.

Griffin in a fancy tuxedo, reaching out a hand to ask me to dance. All the guys from the soccer team pointing and laughing. They can barely look at me, they're so disgusted by the sight of two boys dancing together.

No way my teachers come to my rescue, either. They probably pretend not to notice at all.

I remember when Francis Redmond switched schools last year. The day after he left, it was like he'd never existed. Not a single teacher mentioned his absence.

I make myself breathe.

Desperate to change the subject, I type, *You ready to head to the crystal realm now?*

It's Griffin's turn to go quiet for a minute. I know I deserve that. I'm being rude, not asking him about his dance lessons.

But to be fair, I'm not the one who was trying to bring Oakwood drama into Mirror Realms. This was supposed to be a game, as in the opposite of drama. Why did Griffin have to be friends with Julie anyway?

Okay, Griffin says after what feels like forever. *Sure.*

Then we meet at the entrance to the crystal realm, and we kill so many crystal crabs I eventually lose count.

We earn double the precious gems that we normally would have.

And then I say I have to go because my mom is calling me for lunch, even though that's not true. I actually just want to go.

Griffin doesn't ask whether I might join him and Julie later, and I don't bring it up again, either.

In fact, I don't log in for the rest of the day. Instead, I go back to my room and try to do the makeup work that I missed yesterday, while Dad and I were at Dr. Clarkson's office. Only I barely understand it, because it's all based on stuff that got covered when I was out the time before.

By the second assignment, I'm completely stumped.

I give up.

12

A GOOD AMBASSADOR

There's a mirror that hangs on the back of my closet door. When I finish getting ready and look in it the next morning, I don't like what I see.

Over a stiff collared shirt and a too-tight tie that he only ever wears to church, the boy in the mirror has bright red, puffy cheeks and not one but two acne breakouts— one on his forehead, and one on his chin. This is in spite of the special face wash the boy's mom got him at the pharmacy, during the same trip when she got the boy's steroids. The steroids cause the red cheeks and the acne. The shirt and the tie just make it harder to miss, like putting a party hat on a llama.

Look, I'm not stupid. I know the boy in the mirror is me.

It's just that I don't want him to be, right at this moment. I want to be somebody else.

Maybe it's not really as bad as it is in my head, I decide. Maybe I'm exaggerating things.

But when I join my family on the way out to the car, Dad does a double take at the sight of me. Lexie nearly drops the Saran-wrapped plate of chocolate chip cookies she baked for today's teen group fundraiser. Mom kisses my forehead and says, "I know all this medicine is going to be worth it," and even though she's trying to make me feel better, it just feels like confirmation that I was right to worry.

The real kicker is, the medicine still isn't working. Not enough. Not yet.

All night, I kept thinking about how things went sideways with Griffin, and then my stomach would churn, and I'd have to go to the bathroom, over and over again.

I have half a mind to tell my parents that now. To ask if I can stay home from Weekend Warriors this morning. But if I tell them, then they'll definitely take me back to Dr. Clarkson, who will make me switch to the other medicines she mentioned. The ones with even more serious side effects.

And I know what the boy in the mirror would say about that.

From the first second I enter our Weekend Warriors classroom and find him in the middle of telling a story, it's obvious that Henry is as happy as I've ever seen him.

Henry, when he's happy, gets this energy about him. It's like he can't sit still. He has a smile and a joke for everybody, and the jokes are never mean, like Luca's are. They're actually funny. Sometimes teachers have to tell Henry to settle down, and he's definitely had to go to the principal's office a couple times, but more often than not, even the teachers who are giving him grief have to hide their own smiles behind their hands, where they think we can't see them.

That's why I've always liked being around Henry. It's like his happiness is contagious.

Today, he's telling everybody about Thursday's win against Gordon. From the postgame celebration alone, I've heard the story about ten times already—especially the part where he scored an epic goal with one minute left in the fourth quarter—but it's clear Henry hasn't gotten tired of telling it yet.

Mr. Dyson listens to the story with a big smile on his face.

"Just like in the movies," he says when Henry finishes.

"Everybody pray for us to pull off a win like that in round two," Henry says. "We're playing Pine Mills on Wednesday. They're the top seed in the tournament."

"Surely there are more important things to pray about than that," Yasmin says beside him, but she's smiling, giving Henry a hard time.

I quietly take the open seat on Henry's other side, and he gives my shoulder a shake hello. I haven't told him what Dr. Clarkson and my dad said on Friday, about me not going to away games. Seeing his excitement for Wednesday's game, I'm not sure now is the right time.

"Welcome, Will," Mr. Dyson says. "How're you feeling?"

"I'm good," I say.

"Yeah?"

"Yeah."

"I'm real glad to hear it," Mr. Dyson says.

I can feel him and everybody else in the class taking this chance to sneak a glance at me. Madison's eyebrows go all the way up her forehead. Yasmin offers me a pity wave. Even Henry, still basking in his victory, falters a little in his smile as he turns to actually look at me.

All right, I want to say. *Just get it over with.*

Mr. Dyson starts off today's class with a reminder about the bake sale the teen group is running this afternoon, then opens his Bible to Ephesians, where he says he has another reading from Paul the Apostle.

But Madison's hand shoots up before he can even get to the reading.

"Yes, Madison?"

"I actually had a question about the Corinthians from the other day. Sort of."

"Okay," Mr. Dyson says. "Shoot."

"Well . . ." Madison looks a little nervous, which isn't like her. Since she knows the Bible inside and out, she's usually so confident in here—some might even say a know-it-all (not me, but some). "It's just—I heard that Catholic churches and a lot of Methodist churches don't do gay marriages. And I know this wasn't the passage we read, but my dad says there's another passage in Corinthians about how being gay is wrong. Do you think our church is going to stop doing gay marriages, too?"

"Whoa, okay!" Mr. Dyson says, and he leans back as if he can literally feel the force of her words. "That's quite a big question, Madison, and maybe not the question I was expecting." He sounds even more squirrelly than she did. "You don't have to share if you don't want to, but can I ask where this question is coming from?"

I'm wondering the same thing. Granted, I don't know every single event that occurs at our church, but I've never heard of a gay wedding happening here. I've never even heard of one happening in our town, and in our town, it seems like the kind of thing everybody would be talking about. This town doesn't know the meaning of mind your own business. This town thinks it's one big T-E-A-M.

"Well, my friend, Tab—er, my friend at school—" Madison begins, deciding against saying Tabitha's name a second too late, even though I probably would have guessed she was talking about Tabitha anyway, because they're always hanging out at school—"she has two moms. Sort of. Like, one of them is definitely her mom, and then the other one is the woman her mom married in Atlanta after she divorced her dad."

Mr. Dyson tries to cut in, but Madison keeps going.

"And I was thinking about how you said—well, how the *Bible* said—we need to be careful about bad company because it can make us bad. And I was just wondering if you think hanging out with my friend at school could make me bad, because of her moms? Like, in ways I don't realize? Because my dad says he doesn't like it when I go over to her house. But I think she's one of the nicest people I know. And her moms seem cool, too."

Mr. Dyson takes a deep breath, and so do I.

I guess I wasn't the only one still thinking about that Corinthians lesson from last week. Maybe we're all worried about who's bad company and who's good company.

Before Mr. Dyson can respond, though, Zander—who I don't really know that well because of the homeschooling thing—chimes in.

"The Bible isn't talking about whether someone is nice or cool. The Bible is talking about whether someone is good or bad. There's a big difference. Isn't that right, Mr. Dyson?"

Yasmin answers before Mr. Dyson can. "Gay people aren't *bad*, if that's what you're getting at," she says. "Anyway, Madison, we're Baptist, not Catholic or Methodist. We don't have all the same beliefs as them."

Zander starts to argue. "The Southern Baptist Convention says—"

Yasmin cuts him off. "Our church isn't *in* the Southern

Baptist Convention."

"But in Corinthians—" Madison interjects.

"Okay, okay, let's rein it in," Mr. Dyson says, still smiling, but with an edge of something in his voice that almost doesn't sound like him. Mr. Dyson's comfort zone is "go forth and be awesome." Right now, he looks like a deer going forth in headlights. "Whew. Where to start, am I right? First of all, Madison, thank you for this question. I'm always happy when y'all bring real-world questions into this classroom, because it gives us all a chance to remember that the Bible isn't just a book. It's a light in the dark. It's a living, breathing word."

I try to catch Henry's eye to see how he's feeling about all this, but suddenly it seems like he's making a point of staring at the floor. The Henry who scored last week's winning goal is gone.

"Second of all, I know the passage in Corinthians your dad was talking about, and, uh, well, it's true that a lot of people take it to mean that Paul was speaking out against homosexuality, but plenty of Bible scholars say that what he was really talking about there is, uh . . . how do I put this . . . well, violence against one's fellow man, basically. Anyway, what I'm trying to say is, there's debate there about what exactly was meant by Paul in that particular passage. I'm sure your dad can talk to you more about that, and about why our church isn't part of the Southern Baptist Convention. Only if he's comfortable, of course."

Zander is frowning and looks almost mad, like even this very confusing explanation Mr. Dyson has given has crossed a line somewhere.

Madison considers what Mr. Dyson has said, and she's just about to respond when Mr. Dyson continues. "*Third* of all, I would say that it sounds like you're being a good ambassador and neighbor to your friend at school, who is her own person. Remember what we all learned in Matthew about not judging our neighbors. About *forgiving* others."

Now even Yasmin looks puzzled. I think Mr. Dyson lost her with the idea that Madison might need to "forgive" her friend for having two moms. That's definitely where he lost *me*.

"So, to sum it all up," Mr. Dyson concludes, "that's why I personally always return to the golden rule in Matthew: treat others the way you want to be treated."

No one speaks. It's clear we're all trying to sum it up

for ourselves, at ten different speeds.

Finally, and very seriously, Madison asks, "Even if they're bad company?"

Zander snorts, but he stops himself before he says something that would violate the safe space rule of Weekend Warriors.

"Yes, even if they're bad company," Mr. Dyson says. "You should treat *everyone* with respect. That's the best way to help them to see God's light—through your light. The important thing with the passage we read the other day is just to be mindful of how much you let the bad company change *you*."

There's a word we use in Weekend Warriors, which is a real and true word, but which I've never heard anyone outside this classroom use in my life. The word is "resonate," and Mr. Dyson uses it so much, the rest of us eventually started using it, too. In a nutshell, it means that something someone else has said makes sense to you. But Mr. Dyson said it's more than that. He said that when something *resonates* with you, it means it makes an impact. It feels true. It fills you up like the sound of the church bells that strike every hour.

I can see that what Mr. Dyson has just said has really

resonated with the class. Zander and Madison—even the eighth graders, even *Yasmin*—consider his words like they've finally clicked into some important place. Like they're a real *aha* moment.

I can't tell if Mr. Dyson's speech resonated with Henry or not, because he's still staring at the ground like he's trying to drill a hole into it with his eyes.

But I know this: it didn't resonate with me.

As far as I can tell, Mr. Dyson's whole speech was just a fancy way of saying that it's not Tabitha's *fault* that she has two moms. But so *what* if Tabitha has two moms? If anything, we're the ones who should be asking Tabitha to forgive *us* for dragging her and her family into our lesson like this.

And what's so bad about changing, anyway? Sometimes you can't help that you're changing. Sometimes it isn't your fault, and there's no one to blame.

"Will?" Mr. Dyson says, his earlier smile returning now that he's out of the woods and the class has calmed down. "Penny for your thoughts before we head into today's lesson?"

"I'm good," I say. "Just thinking."

Something in my voice makes Henry finally look up.

He raises an eyebrow and slides his phone halfway out of his pocket, like he's asking me if I want to text him about it. But I don't want to text him. I'm not sure what I'd say.

So I just shrug, at him and Mr. Dyson both.

As the class launches into today's lesson on Ephesians, I find myself thinking about that stained-glass window again. The one from the lock-in. The one that I broke but didn't fix.

In another universe, they never could fix that window. In that broken-window universe, everybody knows it was me.

It's warm enough on this sunny April Sunday that the bake sale is outside, in the little field right next to the parking lot. I call this field the grassy knoll, because Henry called it that one time and Yasmin and I started cracking up. Then the name stuck.

Lexie stands behind the table with six other members of the teen group, doling out homemade cupcakes and cookies to people as they make their way to their cars after Bible study groups. Weekend Warriors was the first group to let out, and Henry already somehow talked his way into a free brownie before he and his parents went home.

Since we all rode over together, Mom and Dad said we all have to stick around until Lexie is finished, which means until all the food is gone or all the people are gone, whichever comes first. In the meantime, my parents are catching up with their friends.

I got tired of the small talk, though, especially since so much of it was about me and my disease. So instead, I'm sitting alone in the car, on my phone.

When I pull up my feed, I see I have a new follow request from a username I don't recognize. It doesn't have a name attached to it—in fact, the username is a string of nonsense letters and numbers—but unlike my account, this one isn't set to private.

I scroll back through this user's pictures, which are almost entirely photos of nature. Sunsets and flowers and weirdly shaped trees. But a little ways down, there's a picture of a very familiar-looking lion's head, and sure enough, when I click through to read the caption, it's from last year: *Serving my best cowardly roar this week #NoPlaceLikeHome.*

This must be Griffin's account.

I start going through the nature photos and realize that most of the captions are references to Mirror Realms.

This orange and blue sunset has a caption about the cloud realm. That fishing pond supposedly looks like it could be the water realm's entrance.

I return to the screen where I can accept or decline Griffin's follow request. I guess I'm glad he's not too mad about yesterday, but the thing is . . . and I'm not proud of this . . . it actually makes me a little nervous to imagine accepting his request.

What if Henry and Luca notice he's following me? What if he starts commenting on my posts? What if he didn't finish saying whatever he wanted to say about the dance yesterday, and now he wants to follow me so he can send me a private message?

There's a part of me that really did want to be his friend that day when I offered him a ride. A part that feels a little braver every time I'm around him, I guess because of his own Oz-given courage. But there's another part of me that feels more afraid than ever. A part that just keeps asking, *Why do you* really *want to be his friend?* Over and over until I feel like a race car spinning out of control on the track.

Things are changing too fast.

I mean, I literally looked like a different person this

morning. And I want to be okay with that. To be okay with me. But I just . . .

It's hard.

I still haven't decided what to do about Griffin's follow request when suddenly the car door opens and Lexie climbs into the seat beside me.

"Question for you: Does Henry ever stop bragging?" she says right away. "I swear, that boy thinks he walks on water. Whatcha doing in here?"

Before I realize what's happening, she's leaning over to look at my phone.

"Hey!" I shout, scrambling to shut it off and get it in my pocket before she can see.

"Whoa, chill out," she says. "What *were* you doing in here?"

Even as I splutter out a response that it is none of her business, the front doors open and Mom and Dad get in, waving and calling goodbye to a few last stragglers, including Dr. Gregory and Mr. Dyson.

"Careful," Lexie says to our parents, "Will is having a meltdown back here."

"What's wrong?" Mom asks, sounding five degrees more serious than the situation requires, probably because she thinks my meltdown is somehow Crohn's related.

"It's nothing," I say. "I'm fine. Lexie was being a snoop."

Dad looks at me in the rearview mirror. I'm pretty sure he winces at the sight of me, just a little bit.

"You all right?" he says.

"I said I'm fine," I snap, and now both my parents turn all the way around in their seats to look directly at me. Lexie has moved so far to the other side of the seat she's practically up against the door.

Mom says, "We know you're going through a lot right now, honey, and the prednisone can't be helping your mood."

I roll my eyes. She and Dad have one of their quick, silent conversations.

Dad clears his throat. "Mr. Dyson told us that Weekend Warriors got pretty intense today. Is that what's wrong?"

I can feel my cheeks burning. *Thanks again, prednisone.*

I'm surprised to hear that Mr. Dyson thought class was intense enough to tell my parents.

"No," I say.

Mom adds, "Because if there's anything you want to talk about, we're here, you know?"

"Yeah," Lexie says, "we're here for you, Will. And we

have the number to the psych ward on speed dial, so just say the word and we'll have the nice men in the white coats come to take you away."

"*Lexie*," Mom admonishes.

But I know she's kidding. We've been making that joke whenever we get in a fight, ever since she took AP Psychology. And something about that return to normal is exactly what I need right now. I actually laugh.

Then Lexie laughs, and the sound of us both laughing makes my mom laugh, too.

Even Dad manages a smile, though I can see he's still worried.

"I'm fine," I say. "Just a little tired."

That answer seems to do the trick. And it's not a lie, either, even if I'm not telling them the whole truth.

They're already worried enough about me. Why give them one more reason to be afraid?

13

TRAVEL JERSEY

At school the next day, all Luca and Henry and the other guys can talk about is round two of the tournament. The game against Pine Mills. One minute, they're all hyped, saying that Pine Mills will definitely be rusty since they had the bye in round one. The next minute, they're saying that Pine Mills will be better rested—unbeatable—for the exact same reason.

I can see they're stressed, but they're excited, too. Normally, I'd be right there with them, obsessing over the what-ifs and but-thens. Not this time, though. Until I can get back on the field, I'm on the outside looking in.

Which brings me to the reason *I'm* stressed. The guys still don't know that I won't be at the Pine Mills game.

They don't know Dr. Clarkson and Dad nixed away games altogether. There was never a good moment yesterday to break the news to Henry, and it only feels harder with Luca here, too.

Finally, there's a lull in the conversation, and I think I've found my moment, but then Henry spots something over my shoulder that makes him frown.

Before I can turn to see what it is, he's already getting up and heading in that direction.

I shift my seat so I can get a better look, and I see Henry making his way toward the far corner of the cafeteria, where Amit is sitting all by himself, eating a lunch that he brought from home. Henry reaches Amit's table, and they exchange a few words. Next thing I know, Henry and Amit are both walking back to our table.

"Hey, guys," Amit says, smiling but not quite meeting our eyes as he sits down.

"I didn't know you were in our lunch period," Luca says. "What's up, dude?"

"Not much," Amit says.

"I was just telling Amit he's always welcome at the soccer table," Henry says with a big smile. He waves his hand in between our starting left fullback, Rashawn, and our other forward, Kent, who are sitting on my other side. "Isn't that right, guys?"

"That's right," they say, nodding hey to Amit before they go back to their own conversation.

"We were talking up the Pine Mills game," Luca says to Amit. "What do you think? We got a shot?"

"Me?" Amit says. "I mean, yeah. I think so. It was close when we played them before, right? So, yeah." He was all confidence and speed on the soccer field last week, but today he's self-conscious. Unsure of himself. I could be wrong, but it seems like he's kind of tripped up on the fact that we saw him eating alone.

"Right on." Henry nods his approval.

"Oh, and Wednesday's a jersey day," Luca says. "Don't forget."

"Wow, thanks, Luca. I would've totally forgotten without you here to help," Henry says sarcastically, flashing a grin for Amit and me.

The joke is that it's jersey day whenever there's an away game on a school day, so it's hard to forget. On jersey day, everybody on the team wears their travel jerseys to school, partly as a team spirit thing but also to quickly show the teachers who is on the team and needs to be released from class early so they can make it to the bus on time.

I think Luca's reminder was really aimed at Amit, but it's so like Henry to step in with a joke to make the new guy feel better. I remember last year when Luca was that new guy, and Henry invited him to sit with us at lunch.

Luca turns to me like he just remembered I'm here, too.

"You're still going to wear your jersey, right?" he asks.

"Why wouldn't he?" Henry answers for me.

"Well, I know Coach said he couldn't be manager, so I wasn't sure if he was riding the bus with us or not."

"Who cares if he's riding the bus or not. He can still wear the jersey."

Amit follows the exchange like it's a tennis match, then looks at me curiously. They're all waiting for me to weigh in. I feel my throat closing up like when I have to make a presentation. I shouldn't be this nervous. I'm only talking to my friends.

"I actually have been meaning to tell you guys," I begin, my voice wobbling annoyingly, "I can't go to the game on Wednesday. My doctor said."

Henry frowns.

"I thought you said you just couldn't play?" he asks, confused.

"Yeah, I'm pretty sure that's what you said," Luca adds (super unhelpfully). "Are you saying you can't go to the games, like, at all?" he presses. "Not even Saturday's game? How does that make any sense?"

It feels like we're standing on opposite sides of a ditch. A ditch so wide it's impossible to cross. Luca and Henry think they're on the right side, but they have no idea what I'm going through over here.

I guess I dug this ditch all by myself. I guess I can't be mad at them for being so far away.

"Listen," I say, "I hate it, too. But my doctor and my dad don't think I'm ready to travel yet. They want me to stick close to home. Better safe than sorry."

"What if you just ignore them?" Luca says. "Maybe if you wear your jersey, we can sneak you on the bus."

I start to laugh, but then I realize he's being completely serious. And worse, Henry looks like he wants me to answer, too. Amit looks totally lost.

"If I ignore them, I could get really sick."

"Couldn't you get just as sick at school?" Luca asks.

"They let you come here, don't they?"

He has a point, I guess. If I'm going to be sick wherever I go, why can't I at least go where I'm happy? But I know it's not totally the same. Principal Baylor told my parents I can go to the bathroom whenever I need to at school, and if things get really bad, I can go to the nurse's office. What am I supposed to do if that happens while I'm on the bus?

The truth is, Luca doesn't understand what it's like when I'm sick. Maybe I *should* explain to him what my Crohn's symptoms are. How serious they can get. Maybe I should send the guys a link, so they can read more on their own, and not just base their thoughts off the he said/she said from the parents at church. But to be honest, I don't *want* them to know more than they already do.

Have *you* ever heard a group of guys get going on diarrhea jokes? They're not really funny on a good day. They're even less funny when the jokes are about you.

It's like Henry can read the expression on my face.

"Dude. Drop it," he says to Luca. "Doctors don't say stuff like that unless it's for a good reason." To me, he adds, "Just get better quick, okay?"

I offer Henry a grateful smile.

"Well, it's going to suck not having you there," Luca says. "You really were our good-luck charm last week. I mean, Amit here might be just the tiniest bit better than you at center midfield, but still, you know what I mean."

He tries to put a friendly arm around Amit when he says this, but Amit looks embarrassed by the attention, so Luca just kind of lets it fall.

"Wow, thanks," I say, feeling pretty embarrassed myself.

"What?" Luca says. "I don't mean it as an insult. Just a fact."

"You're kind of a jerk sometimes," Henry says. "Just a fact."

"Whatever," Luca says, scowling into his lunch.

I'm relieved when the bell rings a second later.

It's not like Luca is wrong. Amit *is* a little bit better than I am. I noticed it myself watching the game last Thursday. I just thought my friends were supposed to have my back on that kind of stuff.

Maybe that's only as long as you're on the same team.

I don't know what this says about me, but even after all that, I still want to wear my travel jersey on Wednesday.

The problem is, it's five minutes before we have to

leave for school, and I can't find it anywhere.

"Mom! Have you seen my travel jersey?" I call from the laundry room.

"I think it's in with the dirty clothes," she calls back.

"It's not! I'm in the laundry room, and I've gone through the dirty clothes like fifty times!"

Mom appears in the doorway. She sees right away that the dirty clothes hamper is practically empty. There's no way I could have missed my jersey if it were in there.

"Did you check in the washing machine?"

I nod. "I've checked everywhere. It's not in my drawers, it's not in my closet, and it's not in here." My voice shakes more with each sentence, and little baby tears prickle at the corners of my eyes. The jersey should be in here, and it isn't. It's such a small, stupid thing, but right now, it feels like the culmination of everything that's wrong in my life.

Which is when I realize that maybe this prednisone really is affecting my mood. No way I would have gotten this upset about a missing jersey six months ago. But then again, all the other stuff wasn't wrong six months ago, so who knows.

"Oh, sweetie, I know," Mom says, pulling me into a hug.

I feel like I'm five years old, but I don't care. Up until Lexie walks by the laundry room.

"Who holds a pity party before eight a.m.?" she says. And then, when I give her my most powerful sister-melting glare, she says, "Kidding!"

Naturally, I run into Luca and Henry in the hall before first period (just in case you thought this was the part where the universe suddenly decides to give me a break).

Henry frowns when he sees me but doesn't say anything. Luca acts like he's talking to Henry, but really he's talking at me: "See? I told you he wouldn't wear it. Good thing you didn't take the bet."

"I couldn't find it this morning," I mumble, but I can see they don't believe me. And now I've let Henry down, since he was clearly sticking up for me behind my back.

The day only goes downhill from there. When Ms. Calhoun asks for our reports from Friday's lab, I realize I completely forgot to finish mine, because it was one of the assignments I didn't understand when I tried to do it over the weekend.

I wait until after class to walk up to her desk and tell her.

"Can I have an extra day for my lab report?" I ask. "I couldn't get the lab to work at home."

Ms. Calhoun sighs and bites her lip.

"I suppose I can give you one more day because of the day you missed. But, Will, here it is Wednesday, and the lab was on Friday. Why didn't you ask me before today?"

I shrug.

"Are you sure you have what you need to figure out the lab tonight?"

I shrug again. Ms. Calhoun gives me a searching look. "Can I give you one teeny piece of unsolicited advice?" she asks. "I know asking for help can be hard, because it means admitting you can't do it all on your own. But sometimes, when you're going through as much as you're going through right now, there's just no way to do it all alone. There's no shame at all in asking for help. But you've still got to ask. Teachers aren't mind readers, even if we wish we could be, you know?"

I nod, less because I know and more because her next class is filing in, and I don't want them to see me getting in trouble.

But her words follow me through the rest of the day. They follow me when I'm not saying anything at lunch, because I feel so bad about the jersey thing, and besides, the only person who seems to notice I'm not talking is Amit. They follow me when I'm not saying anything in fifth-period history, when the announcement comes over the intercom that all soccer players are to report to the bus loading zone, and Kent and Rashawn proudly stand up, flashing their jerseys and earning a few whoops and good-luck wishes from the class.

They follow me when I get home from school and think about logging into Mirror Realms, until—for the third day in a row—I decide to just lie down in my room and listen to music on my headphones instead.

Is it fair to keep avoiding Griffin when he probably has no idea why? Am I expecting him to be a mind reader too, like Ms. Calhoun?

All I know is, it's easy to say I need to ask for more help. But I don't even know what I'd be asking for help *with*.

A tutor in science? I wouldn't need help in science if I weren't missing classes for doctor's appointments.

Can someone help make my medicine work faster so I don't have to take anything stronger?

Can someone help me with the side effects in the meantime?

I just wish things could go back to the way they were. I never needed help with anything before I had this stupid disease.

There's a knock on my door.

"Come in," I say.

Lexie pokes her head into my room. I must have been lying here longer than I realized, if she's already home from work. We're on our own for dinner tonight because Mom and Dad are both going to the parents' group at Wednesday worship. They didn't used to go to that very often, but it seems like they're going a lot more lately.

"Were you looking for your soccer jersey this morning?" Lexie asks, holding it up in her hand.

I jump out of bed.

"Where did you find that?" I say, relief bubbling up inside me.

"It was in the backseat of my car."

I remember now. The week before my colonoscopy, Lexie picked me up from our last regular season game and drove me to Pizza Palace, where a bunch of us from the team were going to celebrate our win. I'd changed shirts before I went in because the jersey was so sweaty, and then Mom picked me up when the dinner was over.

"I was wondering what smelled like blue cheese, but I thought it was just Stewart being Stewart. He's been begging me to clean him for longer than I want to admit."

"Thank you," I say, and wrap Lexie in a hug.

"Okay, okay," she says, but she hugs me back. Right then, the piercing notes of an epic guitar solo punctuate the silence between us. Lexie returns me to arm's length, with a look on her face like she just ate sour candy. "Are you listening to *death metal* in here?" she asks.

Sweet sibling moment: officially over.

14

EDUCATIONAL PURPOSES

Thursday morning, we get our first real rainstorm of the month. The kind of April shower that's supposed to bring May flowers, but that brings a full day of wet socks and rank classrooms in the meantime.

On the bright side, nobody hangs out in the halls on days like this. It's just too gross. That means I'm spared running into Luca or Henry first thing in the morning. Hopefully by lunch they won't be in a foul mood.

I already know the Acorns lost their round two game because Rashawn posted about it last night, with a picture of his frowning face and a caption that just read *L 5–1*. For obvious reasons, I was hoping they'd win. For less obvious reasons, I was hoping that with a win, Henry and Luca would forget about the whole jersey thing and we could go back to normal, or at least normal-ish.

Who knows, maybe they won't be salty about it, considering Pine Mills was the number-one seed and all.

But when lunch rolls around, I quickly get the hint that Luca and Henry don't want to talk about the game. They don't want to talk about much of anything.

Almost as soon as I sit down, Luca sneaks out his phone so he and Henry can start looking at videos of epic skateboard wipeouts. He hides the phone under the table so our teachers can't see it, but that means I can't see it from my side of the table, either. If I tried to get a better view, I'd only draw more attention.

Amit gives me a look of pity, but I'm starting to get the impression he's as slow to make new friends as I am. Neither of us really knows what to say.

At first, I just sit there, waiting for Luca and Henry to get bored.

Then, when they don't, I realize that *I'm* bored. And it's not like I don't have better uses for my time. I mean, for one, I'm drowning in makeup work.

So, I take out my history folder and try to finish the discussion questions that are due today. I didn't get to them last night because the overdue lab report took all my time (and I'm still not sure I understood it in the end).

I groan. Right above the first question, there's a note about how all the answers can be found in a few specific books . . . that I completely forgot I was supposed to get from the library. The rest of the class went to take notes as a group on Friday, when I was at Dr. Clarkson's office. Just one more thing I've missed during my endless run of doctor appointments.

The good news is, you're allowed to go to the library during lunch, as long as you don't bring your food in.

"Hey, guys, I think I need to head to the library to finish this," I say, waving the worksheet in explanation. Amit gives me a thumbs-up, but Luca and Henry barely look up from Luca's phone, even though they definitely heard me. They're acting like I don't exist.

So much for not being salty.

Ms. Steinem, our librarian, helps me find the books I need right away.

I head to the nearest table and race through the questions as fast as I can. I only have about fifteen minutes before the bell rings, so even though I know I'm missing a lot of important information, I don't really have time to care.

Then, as I stuff the worksheet in my backpack and hustle to put the books back on the shelf, I see him.

Griffin.

He's sitting at one of the computers along the far wall, right in front of a window that looks out on the downpour. If anything, the storm has gotten worse since this morning, but besides his Big-Bird-yellow raincoat, Griffin seems oblivious. He's logged into Mirror Realms. How much does he play that game, anyway? He really wasn't kidding when he said he's online all the time.

For one tiny second, I think about sneaking out without saying anything. Just straight-up acting like I didn't see him and heading to fifth period.

Would that be the worst thing?

It's not like we're super-good friends. We were only playing that game together for like a week before he mentioned the dance and things got weird.

Then I think of how it's felt all week, with the guys who supposedly *are* my good friends. Luca and Henry on their side of the ditch, not bothering to include me, even though I hardly need their help to feel low right now.

Not being included really is one of the worst things.

"Griffin," I call out, and he turns in surprise.

"Will?"

"I was just doing some homework for history," I explain. Then I nod at the computer. "Are you on a lunch quest?"

"Ms. Steinem doesn't mind if I play in here, as long as I stick to the building realms instead of the fighting realms. For educational purposes."

"What's educational about Mirror Realms?"

I mean it as a joke, but he says, "There's math involved," so defensively that I suspect he's had to use this justification before.

He looks down at the keyboard. "I haven't seen you on this week."

"There's been a lot going on," I say. "Makeup work and stuff."

"Right, yeah," Griffin says, still looking anywhere but at me. "Well, no pressure, but next time you log into your photo feed, if you see a follow request from a weird username with a bunch of nature photos, that's me."

"Oh, yeah?" I say, kicking myself on the inside. I wasn't lying when I said there was a lot going on this week. So much that I really did forget about Griffin's follow request. No way am I admitting that I saw it and didn't accept him right away. That would make the situation a hundred times worse. "I barely go on there anymore. Here, I'll accept you now."

I pull out my phone and do just that. It takes two seconds. Maybe that's why he's not totally buying what I'm selling.

He gives me a lukewarm smile. "Well, I'd better close out my game before the bell."

He looks at me like that's my cue to leave.

I guess I'm too late. Griffin already feels excluded. How did I mess this up so badly? I was really liking having Griffin as a friend. It wasn't just about Mirror Realms.

It's like my mom always says when someone messes up at the craft store: I'll just have to do some damage control.

"Hey, maybe we can go on a quest this Saturday," I say. It's not like I have anything else going on that day. I'll be stuck at home while the Acorns play in round three of the tournament.

"Yeah, maybe," Griffin says. "Just as long as I don't mention anything about my dance lessons, right?"

Ouch. Okay, so maybe Griffin is a better mind reader than I gave him credit for.

"Griffin, I—I mean—"

"I'm just kidding," he says, although we both know he's not. "It's okay. I'm used to it. None of my theater friends get what I like about Mirror Realms, and none of my Mirror Realms friends get what I like about theater. Not even Julie. This is what I get for being such a weirdo."

"That's not—I mean, you're not a—"

"A weirdo? Please. I have fully accepted my weirdo-ness." He flourishes the sleeves of his yellow raincoat as if to emphasize his point. "Besides, one day, all the things that make me weird around here will be the things that make me cool somewhere else. Somewhere like L.A. or New York."

He sounds so confident. I wish I had half his confidence. Mostly, though, hearing him say that he thinks he'll have to leave here to belong, I just feel sad. Is that really how it has to be?

That's when a voice comes from over my shoulder.

"I *knew* there was no way you were doing homework over lunch."

I already have a sinking feeling in my stomach as I turn to face Luca. He's holding my orange history folder, which

I must have left in the cafeteria in my rush to get here.

"What? No way," I protest. "I really did come here to finish my worksheet." I unzip my backpack and hold it open to him, as if the sight of my worksheet in there proves anything. He barely even glances inside.

"How long have you guys been hanging out?" he asks, looking back and forth between me and Griffin. The way he says it, you'd think he'd caught us doing something seriously wrong.

"I don't know," I mumble.

Griffin looks confused. Does he even know who Luca is? If he did, he'd understand why I'm suddenly freezing up. Why I don't want to say anything more than I absolutely have to.

"You don't know?" Luca says. A smile spreads slowly across his face. He's like a shark smelling blood in the water. "How about this: Was it before or after he asked Henry to the dance?"

Griffin's face turns as white as a sheet of paper. His body goes rigid. He looks exactly the way I feel just before I get sick.

I know I should say something to defend him. I should

tell Luca to mind his own business. Tell him that I've had more fun with Griffin in one week than I've ever had with him, which is pretty sorry, considering we're supposed to be friends.

But I can't bring myself to say that.

I can't bring myself to say anything at all.

My insides are churning, and I feel hot, like I'm standing right under the brightest spotlight in the world.

"I gotta go," Griffin says, not looking either of us in the eye. He scrambles to log out of his game and shut down the computer, and then he gathers all his stuff in his arms.

My voice comes back. "Griffin, wait." I try to catch his shoulder, but he pushes right past us, then takes off at a jog, his raincoat making a frantic *swish-swish* all the way out of the library.

That catches Ms. Steinem's attention, and when she looks back to see what could have possibly made Griffin run out like that, she finds me and Luca. She frowns severely. Suddenly I feel like the worst person who ever lived.

"Oh man, wait until Henry hears about this," Luca

says with a snicker. "He is going to *flip*."

"Dude, seriously? What is wrong with you?"

"Come on, Will, this is hilarious. The dude's making his way through the whole seventh grade."

"What are you talking about?"

"Griffin asked Henry to the dance when they were doing some kind of group project in English. Now he tries to help you with your history homework? If he didn't ask you to the dance already, I'm sure he was just about to. This is like his whole thing."

My head is spinning. I guess I should be relieved that Luca has an elaborate story to explain why whatever is going on in his head is all Griffin's fault, not mine, but it only makes me feel worse. It wouldn't be fair to Griffin if I let Luca go off and lie like that. *I'm* the one who offered Griffin a ride home that day. Not the other way around.

The bell rings to signal the end of lunch, and Luca reaches out to hand me my history folder.

I take a deep breath. "Luca," I say. "It wasn't like that. Seriously. Please don't make this into a big deal."

He looks at me sideways as we head back into the hallway.

"Don't worry," he says, raising his voice instead of lowering it. "I won't tell Henry about your SECRET BOY-FRIEND." He practically shouts those last two words, as if he wants everybody around us to hear him.

"Luca!" I say, and—though I'm not proud of this—I even smack him on the shoulder. Not hard, but still. I'm just so angry that he thinks this is all a big joke.

He stops and faces me. I can tell he's not hurt, but he's definitely surprised. I'm not normally a hands-on guy, even on the field.

"You're seriously upset about this, aren't you?" he says. I don't like the way he's looking at me. Like he's sizing me up. Like I'm someone he doesn't recognize.

"I mean . . . yeah," I say. "Griffin's not how you make him sound. He's all right."

"Okay, then," Luca says, holding up his hands in surrender. "I see how it is. And hey, why shouldn't two guys be allowed to go to the dance together, right? You do you. Love is love."

I want to scream.

He gets to act like this is all so funny, and if I fight back any harder, I'm walking right into his trap.

The worst part is, he could make a big deal out of this without even lying. Without exaggerating one bit. All he'd have to do is tell the soccer team that I started hanging out with a guy who asked Henry to the dance, and then I'd never hear the end of it.

I'd never live it down.

"Seriously, dude, I'm not going to tell the team," he says, smiling at me, like we're both in on the joke again. "But you've got to let me tell Henry. You've got to give me that one."

I swear, I can feel my whole body shaking. I don't see why I have to give him anything, not after that. But all I can hear is that he said he wouldn't tell the team. I feel like I'm walking a delicate line here, and if I say no to him now, he might take that back.

"Okay," I say. "Yeah, you can tell Henry. But *only* Henry."

"You got it, Willie-o."

He flashes me a peace sign, and then he saunters off toward the math hall, where he's in fifth period with Henry. Maybe he'll tell him right away. Maybe he'll wait until soccer practice.

All I know is, the second he's out of sight, it's like all the adrenaline in my body goes out of me in a *whoosh*, and all I feel is stress. Stress and fear. Instead of heading to my class, I run straight to the bathroom. I know I'll get a tardy, but I don't have a choice.

I am seriously sick.

15

THE SHATTERED MIRROR

I only feel worse as the day goes on.

Mr. Hayward is super chill when I'm late to history, and he even lets me be excused, no questions asked, when I have to go to the bathroom again. But the second time I raise my hand, he frowns a little and says maybe I should go see the nurse, which causes the whole class to look at me, like it's my first day back from the hospital all over again.

Julie silently tries to check if I'm okay, but I just shrug at her as I gather my stuff and rush back to the bathroom.

Later, the nurse, Ms. Yolanda, asks if I want to call my parents to come get me, and I shake my head. I tell her it's because I feel all right—I just need a minute—but the truth is, I know if I call my parents, they'll want to run straight back to Dr. Clarkson, who will only increase my meds and forbid me from playing soccer. Maybe for good.

There's a bathroom off the nurse's office, and I use that one more time before I head back for my last two classes of the day.

I focus all my attention on *not* being sick, which means I don't have any attention left for whatever my art and leadership skills teachers are trying to get us to learn. Every time my thoughts start to wander to what Luca might be saying about me at that very moment, I snap my mind back to the present.

Breathe in. Breathe out.

Focus on the sound of the rain.

Today is definitely in the running for worst day of school ever. Even on the bus ride home, everybody stares at me like I'm an alien, facing straight ahead and breathing deep like my life depends on it, because it sort of does.

It's such a relief when I finally get home. I change into sweatpants, warm and dry.

I swear I don't mean to spend the afternoon like I've spent every other afternoon this week—turning out all the lights, then turning up the volume on my angriest rock playlist until I can't hear myself think.

I really do want to say sorry to Griffin. To tell him I haven't been laughing at him behind his back this whole time, the way Luca made it sound in the library.

But when I log into Mirror Realms, Griffin isn't there. At first I feel panicky. Griffin's *always* on Mirror Realms. If he isn't there now, there must be something wrong. Then I remember that today is Thursday. The day Griffin has drama club. I laugh, thinking about how he's in drama club, but I'm the one being dramatic.

And *then* I decide that since I'm already being dramatic, I might as well blast that rock playlist after all. Make it a four-day streak.

Right away, though, it's different.

Today, the music doesn't drown out my thoughts, no matter how loud I make it. Today, it's like the music only makes my thoughts louder. Makes me realize that I'm not just sorry about Griffin. I'm also *angry* at Luca. Why does he always have to put people down like that?

And you know what else? I'm angry at Henry, too. I can't believe Henry would take Luca's side over mine on the whole stupid jersey thing. *Obviously* I didn't forget it on purpose. What kind of best friend gives me the *silent treatment* at lunch, like we're five years old? If he doesn't like this ditch between us, why can't *he* fill it in? Why is it all on *me*?

Plus, if Henry had just kept the whole thing with Griffin to himself, then I wouldn't have to worry about Luca in the first place.

Before I know it, I'm jumping around my room, banging my head to the music, and I'm *really* mad.

Mad at my so-called friends. Mad at my stupid disease. Mad at a world that could give me a disease when I already had enough stuff to deal with in this stupid town.

Did God do this? Did He do this to me?

Crash.

Without even thinking about it, as I was jumping around I pounded my fists onto my closet door. Judging from the sound and the little shards of glass peeking out underneath, I think I knocked the mirror off the other side of the door. I think I broke it.

My bedroom door flies open.

"What in the world is going on in here?" my mom calls out as I scramble to switch off my headphones. "I could hear your music all the way in the kitchen. You're going to lose your hearing listening to it like that." She looks down and sees the mirror shards spilling out from under my closet door. "Oh, Will, what happened?"

"I thought you were at work," I say, and she gives me a look like she doesn't see the connection.

"I took off early. Looks like I got here just in time."

She comes over to me and carefully guides me away from the door. Then she opens it slowly, so the shattered mirror can pour out. I think she can tell I'm already upset enough that she doesn't need to punish me.

"You know, I've never believed in the whole seven-years'-bad-luck thing," she says. "I'll go get the broom."

"Was it a rough day? Or what?" my dad asks at dinner. This is the third time he's brought up the mirror. He's acting like I broke it on purpose. He just can't let it go.

"I guess," I say.

"Do you want to talk about it?"

"Not really." I spin my fork around in my noodles without taking a bite. While the rest of my family eats my mom's amazing spaghetti, a meal we usually have only on special occasions, I'm eating plain noodles and meatballs, with no spicy tomato sauce or parmesan cheese. It seems like everything I eat these days is either beige or brown.

"Is this still about the jersey?" Lexie asks.

"Ugh, I don't want to talk about the jersey anymore either," I say.

"Sounds like a yes to me," she replies. Always the therapist.

Mom and Dad have a conversation with their eyes.

Then Mom says, "I know it's hard not being at the games with your friends."

"Forget those guys," I snap, dropping my fork. "I don't even care about them. May I be excused?"

"But you've barely touched your meatballs," Mom protests.

"And you're not being excused until you tell us what's gotten into you today," Dad says.

"May *I* be excused?" Lexie says, but when my parents give her the same sharp look at the same time, she says, "Okay, never mind."

"I'm just not happy with Henry and Luca right now. Aren't I allowed to be mad at my friends?"

"Of course you are," Mom says. "We just want to know why. We're nosy like that."

I let out a gigantic sigh. They really are.

"They were being jerks to Griffin."

"Language," my mom says, and I shrug. Does she want me to tell them or not?

"Griffin's the one I gave a ride home to that day?" Lexie asks.

"Yeah."

"Why were Luca and Henry being mean to him?" my mom presses.

"Because . . . I don't know."

"No reason at all?" Mom says. "That doesn't sound like Henry."

"Well, I guess he's not Mr. Perfect after all."

"Hmm," is Mom's reply. She and Dad exchange another look.

Dad clears his throat.

"I was actually talking to Henry's dad last night. At the parents' group. He told me that, uh, that a boy named Griffin invited Henry to the spring dance a couple weeks ago. Would that be the same Griffin that Henry and Luca are being mean to now?"

My ears start to burn. *Breathe, Will. Breathe.*

"I don't know. Maybe."

"Maybe?" my dad says, like he doesn't believe I don't know.

"Dad, come on, he clearly doesn't want to talk about it," Lexie says.

"Well that's the whole issue. That's why we have no idea what's going on here."

I'm like a cat that's been cornered, ready to run at the slightest move. I was so worried about what would happen when Luca talked to Henry. I wasn't even thinking about who else Henry might talk to on his own.

My mom cuts in. She's in damage-control mode. "All we're trying to say is that we love you no matter what, sweetie. You know that, right?"

"Um, yeah," I mumble.

"And we know you're going through a lot," she continues, "and that it can be helpful to talk things out when you're in a place like that." She reaches across the table to take my hand, and then she and Dad look at me expectantly, while Lexie stares at her lap.

"There's nothing to talk about," I protest in a small voice.

Dad takes a deep breath. It seems like he's trying really hard to keep his patience in check.

"So it's just a coincidence that you started hanging out with Griffin right when—right when Henry and Luca started being mean to him?"

Right when he asked Henry to the dance. That's what he was going to say, before he changed his mind.

And that's the million-dollar question, isn't it? Why *did* I offer Griffin a ride home from school that day, knowing full well what my friends were saying about him? It was a split-second decision that's caused me weeks of grief, and all for what? After today, I don't even know if Griffin still wants to be friends.

"Will?" Dad says, still waiting for an answer.

"Dad?" I respond, like I have no idea what he means.

"Would it help to talk to somebody else?" Mom asks before my dad loses his temper.

"Like who?"

"I don't know . . . like Dr. Gregory? That's who your dad talks to when he needs a sympathetic ear."

Dad flashes Mom a look, like maybe he didn't want her to share that information with us. She shrugs in response. To me, she continues, "Maybe that would be better than Mr. Dyson, since he's already your Weekend Warriors teacher?"

I dig my palms into my eyes. I know they mean well, and maybe it's like Ms. Calhoun said—maybe I do need help. But from Dr. Gregory? He's the most intimidating man in the world. My only interactions with him are when he's preaching in front of the entire church.

"Why would I talk to him when I don't even know what we'd be talking *about*?"

"Just think about it, okay?" Mom says.

"Fine," I say. "I'll think about it." My parents both let out a breath. "*Now* can I be excused?"

"Sure," Dad says. I think he's as relieved as I am to be on the other side of this conversation. "Now you may be excused."

"Only I wish you'd eat your meatballs," Mom says.

"I'm really not hungry."

Later that night, long after the last sounds of Mom and Dad watching TV in the living room have gone quiet and I'm already in bed, about to go to sleep, there's a knock on my door that's so faint, I almost miss it.

"Come in?" I say.

I'm surprised to see Lexie, in pajama pants and a T-shirt. She closes the door behind her and leans against it.

"Are you asleep?"

"Yes. I'm asleep. I'm just a very good sleep-talker."

"All right, wise guy," she says, coming to perch at the foot of my bed. She looks around my room as she talks, pausing to take in my posters and stuff like she's never been in here. "I just wanted to check to see if you're okay."

"I'm fine."

"Sorry your friends are being jerks," she says.

"Did you come here to say I told you so?"

"What?" she asks, like she's genuinely puzzled.

"I know you've never liked Henry."

"That's not true," she argues.

"Yes it is. You always tell me I need new friends."

"Okay, yes, but I meant you need *more* friends. Not just soccer friends."

"So you really don't have a problem with Henry? Because the way you talk about him sometimes, it really seems like you do."

Lexie thinks for a second.

"Fine, I admit it. Henry's not my favorite. But do you know why?"

"Because he can be full of himself sometimes?"

"Sure, that too. But no, I was going to say something else. Do you remember when we used to play dolls together? I got those two Fashionista Girls for Christmas that year, and you cried because you wanted one, so I let you name one of mine, and then I played Stacy while you played Marguerite?"

"I didn't *cry.*"

"For real?"

"I was, like, six years old."

"Yeah, and you cried like a six-year-old. It's fine. It's normal. The point is, we played with those dolls for months, and you loved them, until one day, Henry came home with you from kindergarten, and you wanted all three of us to play together. He took one look and said, 'Dolls are for girls.' Not mean, exactly. Like he was stating a fact."

I do have a vague memory of this, now that she mentions it. I don't remember it being a big deal. It's definitely not something I've thought about much since then.

"That was one time," I say. "And that was years ago."

"Was it one time, though?" Lexie says.

The thing is, I know what she means. I know there've been times over the years when it was easier to go with the flow and do what Henry wanted to do, instead of pushing for what I might have wanted. I mean, I really do love soccer. No question there. But there are plenty of other things I might like, too. I just don't bring them up, and Henry doesn't ask. I guess it's only gotten more that way since middle school, when Luca started hanging out with us. Now there are *two* flows I have to go with, and they pull me in all kinds of different directions. Sometimes it's hard just to stay afloat.

I don't know. Maybe that doesn't make any sense. But it's clear enough that Lexie can see it, too. So maybe it makes perfect sense.

"I would never say I told you so," Lexie says. "But here's what I will say. I have a good instinct when it comes to people. And that Griffin seemed like a really nice kid."

She gives my hair a quick messing up, and then she goes back to her room.

16

PLEASE SEE ME

Ms. Calhoun kicks off first period by returning a bunch of homework, including my late lab report. It has a C–, a frowny face, and a "please see me" written in red ink at the top. I spend the whole class period dreading that conversation, so I barely hear all the new material about eukaryotic cells vs. prokaryotic cells. Great. I'll probably fail that homework, too.

"Have you thought any more about what we discussed, Will?" Ms. Calhoun says, when I approach her desk after everyone's gone. "I want you to feel like you can ask for help before you get to this point in your work. You know, if you ever need extra help, you can always stop by after school. I'm usually here until four. Or if you'd rather get help from a classmate, you know there's a tutoring sign-up sheet in the library?"

"Yeah, maybe," I say, looking somewhere over her head. She frowns.

"Will, I'm sorry, but if you get another C on a lab report, it could seriously hurt your grade for the class. These are weighted more than regular homework. I think at this point I need to send your parents an email, okay?"

"Okay," I say, though of course it isn't. The last thing I need is my parents' input. They'll think this is all the more reason I need to talk to Dr. Gregory. One more piece of evidence that I don't know what I need myself.

When the bell rings at the end of fourth period, dismissing us for lunch, I hang back, taking extra time to pack all my stuff into my bookbag. I never did hear from Henry last night, which means I have no idea if Luca talked to him, and if so, what he thought. Best-case scenario: he didn't care at all. Maybe he found me hanging out with Griffin a little funny, like Luca hoped. In that scenario, I join them at lunch, and I'm supposed to act like everything's fine. I forget the fact that I'm mad at both of them, and I play along out of self-preservation.

That's the best case.

I head to the library.

Forget Luca and Henry. What I need to do is tell Griffin I'm sorry. That's what good company would do.

Griffin isn't in the library, though.

I check the row of computers, and then I check in between all the bookshelves, as if he might be hiding somewhere with a book. Ms. Steinem watches me suspiciously. I almost ask her if she's seen Griffin today, but I don't think she'd take very kindly to that after yesterday.

Between the bookshelves, where Ms. Steinem won't see me, I take out my phone and pull up Griffin's feed. No posts from this week. I go to send him a private message, then type and delete about ten different versions of a basic greeting. I finally settle on "Hey, you there?"

When he doesn't immediately respond, I head over to one of the tables and try to do some more of my overdue makeup work. The problem is, it's hard to focus, wondering where Griffin might be. I hope he's okay.

Finally, my phone buzzes in my pocket, and I get excited for a second.

It's not Griffin, though. It's a text from Henry.

Where you @? it says.

It's hard to believe he misses me at lunch, considering he ignored me when I was right there yesterday.

His next message sounds more serious:

Lmk when you can talk.

I guess that means Luca told him everything. It doesn't sound like he found it funny after all. Maybe he's decided I'm officially bad company. But that conversation can wait for Weekend Warriors. Today, I just want to make sure Griffin is okay.

By the end of the school day, I still haven't heard back from him. All afternoon, a plan has been forming in my mind, as thoughts of what Griffin might be feeling have spiraled from bad to worse.

I know my bus makes a stop at Loring Street, because it's six stops before the one for my house. And from Loring, it's a pretty short walk to the Reed Street shopping center, where Griffin's mom's bakery, Goldy's, is located.

As soon as my bus leaves the school, I start playing out in my head what I'll say if the bus driver tries to stop me from getting off early. But in the end—maybe because it's Friday, the end of a long week—the bus driver doesn't even blink when I join the line of kids getting off at Loring. I hurry down the steps with my bookbag high on my shoulders, not wanting to push my luck.

The walk is a little longer than I thought, past blocks of solo houses and a few subdivisions, but the good news is, with the sun out today, it's already starting to feel like summer. I still can't believe it snowed just a couple weeks ago, when everything started going wrong. I think part of me is still convinced I haven't woken up from that anesthesia-induced dream.

Finally, I turn the corner onto Reed Street, right into the shopping center. I've been here once before, for the bike store where I picked out my first full-size bike. It was Henry, my dad, and me that day. Henry and I had both asked for bikes for our birthdays, but his birthday wasn't for another couple months. Right away, I was eyeing this red bike near the front of the store. It had seven different speeds, and the owner said the color was called "dark cherry."

"That's the bike I want when it's my birthday," Henry said. I decided I liked a green bike just as well. It had seven speeds, too.

I don't remember Goldy's Bakery from that day. It looks nice enough, but it's not very big—just a couple little tables out front, plus two more visible right inside the floor-to-ceiling windows. There's a glass counter display where I can already see just about every kind of donut you could possibly imagine, and behind that is the wall that must lead back to the kitchens.

I don't see anyone inside at the moment, but when I open the door, an electronic bell chimes, and from the back room, I hear someone call "Coming!" A moment later, a woman appears who I can tell is Griffin's mom as soon as she takes off her hairnet. She has a bright-blond streak, just like Griffin's.

"How can I help you, young man?"

This is the part of my plan that's a little less formed. I was so caught up in sneaking past the bus driver and walking here, I forgot to figure out what I actually wanted to say.

"Hi. Are you Griffin's mom?" I start.

"The one and only," she replies, lighting up at his name. "Are you a friend of his from school?"

"Yeah," I say, even if it might actually be a little complicated after yesterday. "I'm Will. Will McKeachie."

"Oh, Will. You're the poor dear with the stomach thing. Is that right? I was so sorry to hear about that."

"Crohn's disease. Yeah. And no worries. I'm getting used to it."

This last part is a total lie, obviously. I'm not even sure why it comes out of my mouth. I guess I don't want her to feel bad.

"I didn't see Griffin at school today," I say. "I tried to send him a message, but I don't actually have his number. Just thought I'd stop by and see if he's okay."

"Well aren't you a good friend?" She wipes off two flour-covered hands on her apron, then pushes her hair behind her ears. "No, Griffin stayed home from school this morning. I think he caught whatever this bug is that's going around."

"Oh," I say. Suddenly I feel kind of silly for being here. Being out sick is a perfectly logical explanation for not being at school—I would know. And that probably explains why he hasn't responded to my message, too. "Well, could you tell him I stopped by?"

"Absolutely. Do you want his number in the meantime? I'm sure it would make him feel better to hear from you."

I'm not sure if it would or not, but I say, "Sure," and take out my phone. Almost as soon as it's in my hand, it's ringing.

Mom.

I say "excuse me" to Griffin's mom and answer my phone on the second ring.

"Hi, Mo—"

"Where are you, Will?"

I can tell from the edge in her voice that there'd be no point in lying. Getting past my bus driver was one thing. There's no getting past my mom.

"Um, Goldy's Bakery."

"Goldy's . . . on Reed Street? What in the world are you . . . Are you there with Griffin?"

"No. Just me. Long story."

"Well, you'll have to tell me all about it when I pick you up in ten minutes."

"What's wrong? Did something happen at work?"

"No, nothing happened at work. Nothing except that I got an email from Ms. Calhoun saying you're getting Cs in her class, so I decided to come home to spend some quality time with my son. But lo and behold, here comes the bus, and my son's not on it. You can imagine the possibilities that popped into my head."

"Sorry."

"Yes, well, sorry's a start. But it's definitely not the

end. Don't. Leave. That. Bakery. Do you hear me?"

"Yes, ma'am."

"Goodness gracious, Will. I mean, goodness gracious."

I end the call and look back to Griffin's mom, who is watching me with a mix of curiosity and concern.

"Sounds like you gave your mom a scare, huh?"

"You could hear all that?"

She smiles, but it doesn't quite reach her eyes.

"It really was nice of you to come check on Griffin. Tell you what, before I give you his number, why don't you pick out a donut, on the house. Then you can wait for your mom at one of these tables."

17

THE CLOUD PRINCE

My mom buys a half-dozen donuts to say thank you for the free one (and I make sure she gets two of the Nutella donuts I just ate, so I can have at least one more), and then we head back home.

I thought my mom would start lecturing me as soon as we got in the car, but instead she hardly talks, which is almost scarier. Like she's building up to something.

"There's a new *Simon Says Danger* episode we haven't watched yet," she says out of nowhere, when we're a few blocks away from our house. "That could be a fun thing to do tonight."

"Yeah, maybe," I say.

"I thought you liked that show."

"I do."

"You just don't want to hang out with your mom on a Friday night," she says like she's making a joke, but I don't think she is.

"We can watch the show. I just need to get on Mirror Realms at some point tonight. It might even be after dinner."

"You know you're still in trouble, Will. Even if I haven't thought of what to do about it yet."

"It's really important."

She sighs as she pulls into our driveway.

"You and your sister are lucky I'm such a pushover."

"We're usually so well-behaved!" I protest. "We're like model children!"

Mom laughs in spite of herself. She never can stay mad for very long.

"If you say so. Now go on and get inside before I change my mind," she says.

We never do get around to that episode of *Simon Says Danger*. Dad's stuck at work late, Lexie's out with friends, and shortly after Mom and I finally sit down to a dinner of chicken noodle soup and saltine crackers, Mom gets a call from Grandma Jean in North Carolina, and she takes the phone into the other room so they can have a proper catch-up.

Griffin wasn't on Mirror Realms when we first got home, but maybe he's on there now.

I hope he is.

I head to the den and fire up the computer. I reach the Mirror Realms login screen where Willnot, my Healer, is waiting, and I swear he gives me a look like he knows I've been a bad friend this week. His unibrow is creased in a disapproving scowl.

I click to my friends list as fast as I can, but when I do, the letdown is immediate. Still no Griffinlord13.

Then I remember that I have Griffin's phone number now. It was really nice of his mom to give it to me, considering she'd just learned I'm a bus-hopping delinquent.

Even though it makes me a little nervous, I send Griffin a text.

Hey—this is Will. Your mom gave me your number.

After a minute, he responds.

Yeah, she told me.

Okay, so he doesn't sound thrilled to hear from me. On the other hand, he responded. That's a good sign, right?

Did you really go to my mom's bakery just to check on me? he asks.

Yeah. And for the Nutella donuts, I joke. I hesitate for a moment, and then I add: I feel so bad about yesterday.

He sends a shrug emoji. Doesn't say anything else.

Do you want to play Mirror Realms? I ask. I'm on there now.

When he doesn't respond right away, I figure I have my answer. And I know I deserve it after not standing up for him when it counted yesterday. If he never wants to be friends again, that's his choice to make. But then I hear the trumpet sound of a friend logging in, and I get a pop-up message from Griffinlord13.

It says: *I'm lighting a beacon if you want to join.*

Be right there, I respond, glad he can't see how big my smile is in real life.

I check the map, and sure enough, there's a dot of light in the cloud realm, marking Griffin's location for anyone on his friends list. The cloud realm is very high level, and I'm not likely to be much help if he wants to go questing there, but I equip the best armor and weapons I have (all of which Griffin gave me) and teleport to the beacon location.

I appear right next to Griffin's blue-skinned Fighter, standing in the center of a cloud that's so high above the other clouds, it'd be impossible to get here by jumping. I wonder if someone else lit a beacon for Griffin, or if he somehow got up here on his own.

Below us, I see players of all three classes battling cloud monsters that shoot lightning bolts. Judging from the number of explosions, the monsters are as intense as I feared. Up here, though, we're safe. I like this cloud Griffin found.

Is this your spot? I ask.

One of them. I have a lot, for when I don't feel like fighting.

That makes sense, I say. Then, because it turns out I'm just like my dad and I can't let things go, I add: *Like the library at school?*

lol, he says.

Translation: he doesn't want to talk about it.

Were you really out sick today? I ask instead.

I mean . . . mental health, but yeah.

He needed a mental health day. That's how bad it was yesterday. On some level, I already knew this, but it still hurts to hear. Guilt lodges in my throat like a piece of unchewed food.

Do you feel better? I ask.

He responds with another shrug emoji.

I got this cool Cloud Sword in a random drop this morning, he says, and his Fighter brandishes a weapon that looks like it's made of air.

Sweet, I say.

So not all bad, he finishes.

Does your mom think I'm a lunatic?

No way! She loved you, he says, adding a smiley face. *Oh, hey, Julie just got on. Going to light a beacon for her, too.*

Cool, I say.

And I guess it's cool. I don't know how much Julie talks to Henry. At least in history today, she didn't act like anything was up. But so much for getting a chance to tell Griffin sorry, or any of the other things I logged on here to say. Still, if Griffin wants a group hangout on his mental health day, who am I to say no?

In a flash of light, a Scholar character appears on

the cloud with us, looking like some kind of angel with flowing robes and a tiara made out of daggers. You can tell Scholars apart from Healers and Fighters because of the dark purple light that swirls around their hands—it's the sign of their magic. Julie's magic looks strong.

I get a pop-up message telling me that Lady_J has entered the chat and would like to add me to her friends list. I quickly accept.

Willnot. I like it, she says in greeting.

What do you think? Should we try to save the Cloud Prince? Griffin asks. I have no idea who the Cloud Prince is, but if Griffin thinks I'm going to survive a fight down there, with those lightning-shooting monsters, he's more of a lunatic than I am.

Let's do it, Julie says. *It's the only way to get the cloud-shark dance.*

Cloudshark . . . dance? I have no idea what that is, but I have a more pressing question:

Is it okay that I'm only level ten? This realm looks intense.

Just stick close to me, Griffin says. *Focus on heals, and Julie and I will protect you.*

Focus on heals. I like the sound of that.

Over the next hour of playing, I get the answers to all

my questions. At least the ones in-game. Cloudsharks are exactly what you'd get if you crossed hammerheads with hawks, and they swim through the air, flapping their wings while wiggling their bodies. Five of them are guarding the Cloud Prince's tower, possessed by some evil NPC Scholar who's making a play for the throne. When we finally free the prince (no thanks to me—despite sticking to our strategy, I die, like, fifteen times), he gratefully gives us a thousand gold pieces each and a cloudshark dance add-on. Now, when I press Ctrl + XZ, Willnot flaps his arms and wiggles his body, just like—you guessed it.

It's pretty hilarious.

Will, you're a natural! Julie says.

It's just three buttons.

Not the dance, she says, adding a laughing emoji. *The healing. lol.*

Yeah, Griffin adds, *we could NOT have done that without you.* Maybe I'm the last person in the world to figure this out, but it feels good to hang out with people who are genuinely nice. People who aren't constantly trying to one-up each other by putting each other down.

It's also nice to be able to spend time with friends without leaving my house. In a place where the side effects of prednisone don't matter, because I can pick how I look.

I'd almost forgotten what hope feels like, but I think it feels like this. It's funny how hope for the future is something you feel in the present, based on a memory of something you've felt in the past.

Then, Julie asks, *Will I see you at the game tomorrow, Willnot?*

Suddenly, all that stuff I managed to forget in the real world for the last hour comes crashing back. The championship tournament. The team. Henry and Luca, especially.

I guess this means she hasn't talked to Henry. At least, not about me. Does she even know about Griffin asking Henry to the spring dance? What does Griffin think about the fact that she and Henry are going together?

Oh, gosh. The spring dance. It's exactly one week away.

Breathe, Will. Breathe.

My doctor says I can't go to the games for now, I say.

Wow, I'm sorry, Julie says. *Hope you feel better soon.*

I hope so, too. But I'm starting to wonder if that's ever going to happen. Crohn's has no cure, right? And I'm already taking the heavy artillery. Maybe this is just how it's going to feel, from here on out.

"Will, my man, don't you think you've been on that thing for a while now?"

It's my dad. I didn't even hear him get home—I was so caught up in this game.

"Let me just tell them good night," I say.

"Them?"

"Some friends from school."

It looks like he's about to ask me a follow-up question but then decides against it. I tell Griffin and Julie I have to go, and Julie says she was about to log off anyway.

Griffin just sends a goodbye-wave emoji.

I wonder how long he stays on after we leave.

Henry texts me again while I'm getting ready for bed.

??? You sick? Or just ignoring me?

Good, I think bitterly. Now he knows how it feels.

18

FAMILY DAY

Mom knocks on my door bright and early the next morning.

"Wake up, Will! I've got a surprise for you!"

I head out to the kitchen, still wearing my pajama pants and rubbing my eyes. Lexie is here too, looking every bit as tired as I am.

"What's all this about?" she says. "I was out way too late for this."

"Yes, and we're going to have a talk about that later," Mom says. "But today is family day! No arguing or fighting all day long."

"Is that the surprise?" Lexie says.

"What's 'family day'?" I ask.

"Family day is something I was reading about on one of my blogs. It's supposed to be a chance for everyone to unplug from electronics and reconnect as a family."

"Does Dad not have to join?" Lexie asks.

"I heard that," Dad says, coming in from outside and holding three huge bags from McDonald's in one hand. "And no, I don't *have* to join. I *get* to join. I think this is a great idea your mom had, and I for one am looking forward to it."

Lexie catches my eye and then twists her finger around her ear, making it look just enough like she's like twirling her hair that our parents won't realize she's calling them cuckoo.

My mom loves to get ideas from her craft blogs, all part of what she calls "going back" to her "creative well." So that part doesn't surprise me. But:

"Why today?" I ask. "I'm kind of drowning in makeup work at this point. I was finally planning on catching up today."

"Come on, bud. There'll be time for that tonight, and tomorrow, and the rest of your life. Maybe we can even look at some of that work together, after we do the other stuff your mom has planned."

"Please no," Lexie says. "I did seventh grade once, and that was more than enough."

"Listen, my beautiful, wonderful children who I love so much, the whole point of family day is that we *all* have a lot of work, and it's been keeping us in our little separate bubbles, and I don't even know half of what's going on in this house anymore. Will's getting Cs in chemistry and going who-knows-where after school, Lexie is staying out way past the curfew we agreed upon—"

"Mom, I said I was sorry," Lexie tries to cut in.

"—and Grandma Jean tells me she's feeling lonely and we don't call her enough, and you know what: she's absolutely right."

With his free hand, Dad traces a comforting circle on Mom's back. I get the impression they talked about this last night, when they were cooking up this "surprise."

"So!" Mom says. "Family day! Now go get dressed."

It seems nobody wants to be the first to move.

"Um . . . can we eat first?" Lexie says.

"Fine," Mom says. "Yes, let's all eat breakfast together at the table. As a family. *Then* go get dressed."

"Will, I got you pancakes," Dad says. "Those are safe, right?"

"Yes, sir," I say.

I decide now is not the time to remind everyone that Mom's pancakes are a million times better than McDonald's, even if it's a compliment.

I think the first rule of family day is to not rock the boat.

After we all eat and get dressed, Mom's next idea is for us to help her pick out photos to put in a new scrapbook to send Grandma Jean. Mom loves to make scrapbooks, and I *know* she's made some for Grandma Jean before, but I guess old people can never have enough family photos.

Mom gets out her thumb drive where she stores all her photos, sorted by year, then month, then event. At first, it's sort of fun going through pictures of stuff I forgot, like the time we walked through the underwater tunnel at the Georgia Aquarium, and fish swam all around us, just like cloudsharks.

But the more my mom oohs and aahs over how cute Lexie and I were in this and that old photo, the more I start to feel like it's in contrast to how I look now, with puffy red cheeks and acne that gets worse every day.

And really, there's only so much looking at photos four people can stand.

The next activity is Dad's idea, and in my opinion, it hardly counts as family day worthy, but Dad argues there's nothing in the rules that says the activities can't also be useful. So we all have to sort through piles of stuff he set aside for us to either keep or put in a yard sale when he cleaned the garage. I vote to keep my old Legos but sell my old baseball cards.

Then it's on to picking out a dance from TikTok for the whole family to learn. I think this might have been the original seed for the idea, since Mom already has three options ready to go. Lexie points out that we were supposed to be unplugging from electronics today (I guess she didn't get the memo about the first rule of family day).

"Just one dance," Mom says. "If it's not fun, we'll scrap it."

I guess I just have cloudsharks on the brain, because I swear the dance we pick isn't all that different from the full-body wiggle. Mom and Dad can do it surprisingly well, but Lexie and I are both so embarrassed by the sight of our parents dancing like teenagers that we can barely get through the choreography ourselves.

"Please do not post that anywhere," Lexie says, when we finally finish a take of all four of us that looks decent.

"Oh, please, please, please," Mom says. "What if I just post it for my close friends list? Your aunt Bev will die. We used to do dances like this when we were girls."

"Fine," Lexie says, and I give Mom a thumbs-up to show my approval as well.

After all that, it's still somehow only midmorning when we hop in the car and head to what Mom and Dad swear will be the best part of the day and the real surprise.

Lexie and I figure it out about two minutes before we arrive, because we turn into a shopping center that includes a grocery store, a phone store, a car wash, and an escape room place, and we figure we're probably not going to have a picnic while our car gets cleaned.

Instantly, I'm excited. I really have been wanting to do an escape room for a while. I thought of it as a potential birthday party idea, right *after* my birthday last year, when we went to see a new superhero movie that wasn't very good.

Even Lexie perks up for the first time all day.

"And you said your mom and dad never have any good ideas," Dad says.

"No one ever said that," Lexie says, but she's smiling.

We head inside and check in at the front desk, with a guy whose name tag identifies him as *Frederick R.— Senior Escape Artist*. He gives us a lock for a locker where Mom and Lexie can put their purses and all of us can leave our phones. You don't have to leave your phone, but Frederick says it's more fun if you do the puzzles without it, and Mom tells him that's perfect, because we're trying to unplug today.

"Excellent," Frederick says. "Just give me a couple minutes to set up the room, and then I'll lead you right in."

We appear to be the only family here at the moment, but I'm still relieved to see the bathrooms are single-user. Even though pancakes were a safe bet for breakfast, my stomach feels unsettled. I don't know if it ever fully recovered from this stressful week. Since we're about to be locked in a room for an hour—that's kind of the whole point of an escape room—I'm hoping I can avoid getting sick for at least that long.

"Right this way, McKeachie Clan," Frederick says, leading us through a hallway and into a room that looks like a mini museum, with paintings on the walls, and with insects, animal skeletons, and more behind thick plates of glass.

"Welcome to the Georgionian Museum, which puts the Smithsonian and the Louvre and all those other museums you've heard of to shame. As of this moment, you are no longer an ordinary family. You are the infamous McKeachies, international art thieves. You are here at the Georgionian Museum because they've just unveiled a previously unknown painting called *Mona Lisa's Niece*. It's worth a fortune, but it's kept under tight security."

Frederick says this all in a very dramatic voice. I wonder if he's into theater like Griffin.

"To make matters more complicated," Frederick continues, "you've heard from your contacts that the painting on display *might* be a forgery." He motions to a door that leads farther in. "So, even if you can make it into the room where the painting is on display, you'll need to be sure that you have the real thing. Once you're sure you have the right one, you'll need to escape the museum without getting caught.

"You'll have sixty minutes. And if you get stuck on anything and need a clue, you can just push this button over here to access a direct line to me at the desk. You'll get three clues total."

My dad puts his arm around me. "What do we do if we need a bathroom break in the middle?" he says. My face grows hot, and I swear Frederick addresses his answer directly to me, because Dad makes it so obvious I'm the reason he's asking.

"In case you need to leave the room for any reason, this door you came in through will remain unlocked the whole time. Because you're on a timer, though, I recommend that you use the restroom now if you need to."

I can see Dad getting ready to explain why that might not be possible, in case that buys us extra time or something. I quickly nudge him in the side to let him know I don't want him to say anything. It's too embarrassing.

Dad seems to get the message. He says, "That sounds good, then. Thank you."

"If there are no other questions?" Frederick says.

We all shake our heads.

"Your sixty minutes start now." Frederick closes the door behind him, and right away, the TV screen on the far wall lights up with a countdown clock, showing the time we have left.

We all split up and start examining the room, calling out to each other when we encounter a puzzle, because the solution might be closer to someone else. We're trying to find the combination to a lock that will lead into the next room, but we quickly realize that each number in the combination will come from a different challenge, and then we'll have to put them all in the right order at the end.

With about forty minutes left on the clock, we get a good rhythm going. Mom lists all the colors of the butterflies in a case so that Lexie can put four paintings with matching colors in the same number order on the wall. Meanwhile, Dad uses a loose rib from the dinosaur rib cage to fetch a key from an empty aquarium—a key that will unlock a small chest across the room. I've figured out that I'm supposed to use the first letter of each precious gem in a jewelry box to spell out a word that will unlock a different small chest.

The only problem is, I don't know what kind of gem

this orange one is, and I'm determined not to use one of our three clues yet. I know we'll need them for the harder puzzles in the next room.

I'm just about to ask if any of my family members know of any orange gems when I feel that awful churning in my stomach. That urgent feeling that tells me I need to get to a bathroom—fast.

"I'll be right back," I call to my family, and they all look up with worry, my mom asking, "Are you okay?" and clearly losing her place with the butterflies in the process.

"I'm fine—just keep going," I reply, and I can't really stop to explain beyond that. I get to the bathroom just in time.

When I come out, expecting to run right back and pick up the gem puzzle where I left off, I'm stopped short by the sight of my family standing in the waiting room.

"What happened?" I ask. "Did you beat it already?"

"Are you okay?" Mom says, coming over and putting her hands on my shoulders. I notice she's wearing her purse again, like they've already cleaned out the locker for some reason.

"I'm fine," I say, gently shrugging off her hands. "Come on, our clock's still ticking."

"Will . . . ," Dad says.

"Don't worry," Lexie says, waving an envelope, "he gave us a voucher so we can come back another day when you're feeling better."

"What?" I say.

"Truly, it's no problem," Frederick says from behind the desk. "We're happy to have you back any time."

I try to smile and say thank you, but I'm so mortified, I don't think any actual human words come out. Suddenly I want to be as far away from this place as possible. I can't imagine coming back if it means having to face Frederick again.

I turn and make my way to the car as quickly as I can, my family following behind me.

We're driving in silence for a few tense moments before Dad says, "Was it the McDonald's?"

"No, I'm pretty sure it was the Crohn's disease," I say, full of sarcasm.

"*Will.*"

"Why couldn't we just finish the room?" I say, louder than I mean to. "Why did we have to make it a big thing?"

"Sweetie, we did keep going at first," Mom says. "But you were in the bathroom for fifteen minutes."

"No way," I say.

Mom turns back to me, her expression sad. Of course they would know. There was a clock counting down right there on the wall.

She hands me my phone out of her purse.

"That room would have been hard enough with all four of us," Lexie says. "Anyway, it's no big deal. We'll steal that fake painting next time."

"It *is* a big deal," I say. "How am I ever supposed to figure out how to live with this disease if y'all just keep making my decisions for me? First it was no playing soccer, then it was no going to away games. Now I can't even get through family day? I can't do anything anymore!"

Mom's lip quivers like she's going to cry.

"Great job, Will," Lexie says.

"No, no, I get it," Mom says. "He's upset. And you know what, Will, you're right. We *all* have to figure out how to support you with this. If your dad or I could have this disease instead of you, we would swap with you in a heartbeat. But since we can't, we're just trying to do everything we can to protect you."

"Maybe I don't want to be protected."

"Well, then I guess we'll keep making your decisions for you, since you don't seem to know what's in your own best interest," Dad says.

Mom sucks in a breath, and Lexie whispers "Dang" so low I immediately wonder if I imagined it. Dad's declaration hangs heavy in the air. Even he seems to realize that it came out harsher than he meant it. He keeps looking at me in the rearview mirror with concern in his eyes.

I refuse to let him see me cry, but it's hard, to be honest.

This is why I don't tell them anything. It's hard to trust them when they don't trust me.

All I know is, whether it's my fault or not, the boat has officially been rocked. Some family day this turned out to be.

Dad tries to lighten the mood, or at least break the silence.

"I bet the Easton game is over by now. Have you heard from any of your friends how it went?"

I realize he's right, and in spite of the fact that I want

to stay mad at him, my curiosity is stronger. I check my phone.

No new messages. I guess Henry finally gave up on me.

Then I head to my feed, and once again, Rashawn has come through with the postgame results photo.

It's all my teammates, jumping for joy on the field. Caption: *W 2–1*. So it was another close one.

"They won," I say. "The Acorns are still in it."

19

PASSING AND DRIBBLING

When Mom knocks on my door the next morning and says it's time for church, I tell her I'm staying home. I need a mental health day.

"You what?"

"A mental health day. It's like a sick day for my brain."

"I don't know, Will . . ."

"Ask Lexie. They're a real thing."

"I know they're a real thing," Mom says. "I'm not questioning that. I just think that if you're feeling down, going to church will help you feel better."

"Henry and I are still fighting. And I'm feeling stressed after our big day yesterday."

Mom lets out a gigantic sigh. I can see she's on the fence. I also know that after Dad's accidental outburst in the car, he and Mom are treating me with kid gloves again. I'm not above playing the family day guilt card if it gets me out of Weekend Warriors.

"Fine," she says. "But just this once. After today, you and Henry are going to have to find a way to get along."

Relief washes over me. The truth is, my stomach actually hurts worse this morning than it did yesterday. But if I was starting to think about finally coming clean and telling my parents that my medicine hasn't been working this week, yesterday completely changed my mind. If I tell them now, they'll never let me be the judge of my own health, ever again.

And to be fair, all of this *is* affecting my mental health, too.

I'm not totally lying.

But it turns out I was wrong when I thought Henry had given up on me. And unlike my mom, he apparently didn't think it could wait another day.

That afternoon, when my family is back from church

and I'm puzzling over my ever-growing mountain of makeup work, Dad stops by my door and says, "Henry's here to see you."

"Henry's . . . here?" I repeat. "Like *here* here?" Asking the same question twice: another classic stall tactic.

"At the front door. I invited him in, but he said he could wait outside."

My dad looks at me like maybe I'll clue him in as to what's with all these weird vibes between Henry and me. Yeah, no thanks. He'd probably call an exorcist.

"Okay, I'll be right there," I say, trying to sound more confident than I feel.

When I step outside a moment later, I find Henry standing in the driveway, next to his bicycle, the dark-cherry finish glistening in the sun. His kickstand's not even down, like he's ready to bolt. But he doesn't look mad like I thought he would. He looks . . . I don't know, worried? It's hard to say. I've never seen this expression on Henry before.

"Hey," I say, joining him in the driveway.

"Hey," he replies.

We stand there for a minute, neither one of us speaking.

He's the first one to crack. "Did you hear we beat Easton?"

"Yeah. I saw Rashawn's post."

"Right," he says.

"So who are you playing Tuesday? Do you know yet?"

"B-Prep."

B-Prep is what we call Brookside Preparatory Academy. It's the private school where Francis Redmond transferred last year. We beat them 3–1 in the regular season, and I was so relieved, because two of the eighth graders on our team had been trying to get everybody to hold up limp wrists going into the postgame high fives, and the idea might have caught on if we'd lost. (I couldn't believe they'd held a grudge for a whole year. Francis wasn't even wearing his rainbow socks in the game.)

"Well, good luck," I tell Henry now.

"Dude, are we cool?"

The question catches me off guard. It's so like Henry to just come right out and say whatever's on his mind. And it's so like Henry to act like this is all on me.

"I don't know," I say. "Are we?"

"Julie came to the game yesterday. She said you two

were playing some video game Friday night? Is that why you didn't text me back?"

"I just haven't been feeling well."

"*Right*," he says, with a sarcastic scoff.

"Wow, okay. I know you and Luca think Crohn's disease is basically a stomach bug, but it's actually a pretty serious disease."

"I don't think it's a stomach bug," Henry protests. "I actually read all the symptoms and stuff on Google. It sucks, dude. I know. Is that what this is about?"

Wait, he looked up my disease on Google? Why didn't he tell me?

"I mean, not really," I mumble, a little deflated now without my anger.

"Then what? 'Cause you're obviously ignoring me. You didn't even come to church."

Part of me wants to say, *You ignored me first*. But it sounds so babyish, even in my head. And it's not the real issue, is it? That's not why there's this deep ditch between us.

"You know what," I say quietly.

Henry sputters out a few nonsense words, like he wants to keep arguing. But I can see the moment the anger goes out of him, too.

"I never should have told Luca about Griffin asking me to the dance."

"Why did you?"

"I don't know, dude. It was just so random." Henry runs his hand through his hair, debating how much he wants to get into this. "Like, that weekend, I was doing this English project with Griffin at my house, where we had to make a commercial for this Shakespeare thing. And there's a dance part in it, so after we finish, we're laughing and cutting up about how the spring dance has gotten out of control, with all these over-the-top invitations and stuff. There's so much pressure on who you go with. All the videos and the likes and just all of it, you know? I hate it. So much."

Henry grinds his toe into the driveway, punctuating his point. He's looking everywhere but right at me. "Anyway, we were talking about that. So then Griffin asks me, do I have a date? And I say—just kidding around—'Why, do you want to go with me?' And then he says, 'I would if you would,' just like that. Absolutely *not* kidding. Stone-cold serious. I didn't know what to say. I was like, whoa, dude—sorry, I'm flattered, but wrong idea. And he got completely embarrassed. He just up and left. Edited the project at home."

My head is spinning around in circles. It's like I can picture it all so clearly, and at the same time, I can't really picture it at all. How does someone just . . . ask that?

I also didn't know Henry felt pressure around the spring dance. He always seems so at ease with himself.

"What does that have to do with Luca?"

"So yeah, you weren't at school the next day. You were out for your telescope thing."

My *colonoscopy*.

"But I had to tell somebody. I just felt so bad. It felt like—I don't know. Maybe I led Griffin on? So I asked Luca at practice. But he totally went off. I know how he gets, okay? I know he can be a lot."

"That's one way of putting it."

"It was a mistake. I own that. But I made Luca swear he wouldn't tell anybody else. I was so mad when he told you, even. No offense."

"Okay. Except then you told your dad, who told my dad. And now my dad wants to know if it's only a coincidence that I started hanging out with Griffin after all that."

Henry's eyes go wide.

"Wait, seriously?"

I look back at my house. Make sure the front door's still closed and the blinds are still down.

"Seriously."

Henry toes a circle in the driveway. I can tell he feels bad, but I don't really think it's my job to make him feel better. Not about this.

Finally, with his eyes still on his shoes, he says, "Well, is it?"

"Is what?"

"Is it a coincidence? Luca said you acted like Griffin was helping you on some assignment. But I didn't think you guys had any classes together."

"Luca doesn't know what he's talking about," I snap. "He sees whatever he wants to see."

"Okay," Henry says. "It's just . . . you sound awfully defensive."

"That's because you guys are teaming up on me!"

Henry sighs.

"I'm not trying to team up on you. I'm just trying to figure out what's going on up there." He taps on the side of his head. What he means is: he wishes he knew what I was thinking. I almost tell him, *Join the club*.

"Mom said I should talk to Dr. Gregory," I finally say. If anyone will understand why I might as well talk to the president of the United States, it's Henry. He was there when I broke that stained-glass window. He heard the sermon where Dr. Gregory talked about how hard it was to fix.

But Henry surprises me.

"What's so bad about that?" he asks.

"Really? I mean, he's *Dr. Gregory.*"

"Dr. Gregory's cool. Have you seen his car?"

I shake my head.

"Dude drives a silver Jag. Seriously. My dad says it's vintage."

"Okay," I say. I don't really see what that has to do with anything. I guess Henry can tell from my reaction that I'm not impressed.

He scrunches his eyebrows.

"Are you afraid he's going to say you can't hang out with Griffin anymore because he's gay?"

"We don't know Griffin's gay," I say, like some kind of reflex.

Henry gives me a look that could turn milk into butter.

"He could be pan or bi or something," I insist. "Like Francis Redmond."

This statement hangs in the air between us, and my adrenaline spikes, even though I'm standing still. I worry I've already said too much. Revealed just how much I've been thinking about this.

But Henry says, "Well, I still don't think Dr. Gregory will care, even if he's all of the above. That's not his style."

Finally, my brain catches up to what Henry's putting down. The real reason why he biked all the way here, when he could've just texted.

I think Henry's trying to fill in the ditch.

I hope he's right about Dr. Gregory. Either way, though—I'm a lot less worried about Dr. Gregory, now that I know where Henry stands.

"So . . . you don't think he'd tell me I'm being messed up by bad company?"

"Nah, man. You're good company. Dr. Gregory knows it. And if you say Griffin is good company, then that's enough."

I wonder what Madison's dad would say about that. Or Zander. Or even Luca. I know Henry can't speak for all of them, but he can speak for himself.

And for the moment, that's enough.

❋ ❋ ❋

I get the soccer ball out of the garage, and Henry and I kick it around the front yard, not going all out, just passing and dribbling.

It feels so good to be kicking the ball again. Even like this.

By the time I realize the sun's starting to go down, my mom pokes her head out the front door and says it's almost time for dinner. She asks if Henry would like to join us before she gives him a ride home, but he says he'll be fine on his bike.

When it's just the two of us again, and Henry's got his helmet on and his foot on the pedal, he says, "You think your doctor's going to let you come to the dance?"

"I don't know," I say. The truth is, I still don't know if I want to go either way. I wasn't exactly looking forward to it, and now everything with Luca and Griffin has made me dread it even more.

"Well, if you, uh, don't have other plans, you're welcome to join Julie and me for dinner just before. Luca might join, too, and Ashley—if Luca ever gets around to asking her."

"Thanks," I say, and then Henry heads for home.

I don't know if I've totally forgiven him for ignoring me last week, but it *is* nice to be included. To feel like part of the same team again.

"You were out there for a while," my dad says when I come in. He's sitting in the living room, in the chair that faces the door. Behind him, he has the news on mute.

"Sorry. I lost track of time."

"No, no, I think it's good. How do you feel?"

"Fine. I mean, good."

"Come here. Sit for a second." He motions to the chair beside him, and I perch on the edge of it, unsure. He doesn't talk right away. "You really miss it, don't you?"

"What, you mean soccer?"

"No, I mean the cold weather. Yes, soccer." He's smiling, like he thinks I was giving him a hard time on purpose. (To be fair, I was.)

"I've been thinking about what you said yesterday," he continues, "about letting you make decisions for yourself. You know I'm all about safety first. Hope for the best but plan for the worst—that's what my dad always used to say. But in your case, I think you might be right. The worst has already happened. Now what we've got to do is plan how to live with it. What to do next."

"Okay?" I say it as a question. He clearly already has a plan in mind.

"Well, I was looking at my calendar, and it's pretty clear on Tuesday. If you think you're ready to play in the next game, I'd be happy to take off work and come watch."

"Really?" I almost can't believe it. The only way I know this is my dad and not some mind-controlling brain slug is that of course my dad would clear his calendar for Tuesday, and not just wait for the championship game this weekend. He knows as well as I do that there's still a strong chance this could be Oakwood's last game of the tournament. B-Prep could easily win.

"You bet."

My stomach turns over, as if it thinks I forgot about it. I slump down in the chair.

"It's just . . . I don't think I'm ready to play again yet."

"Are you sure? Henry was here, what, forty-five minutes? Almost an hour? Maybe you could play one half, and that new center could play the other."

"His name's Amit," I say. "And honestly, he can handle both halves on his own. Henry and I were just passing it back and forth. It's the running that's the real problem."

"Right. Yeah, of course," Dad says. "That's very mature of you, son."

"Maybe we could go to the game, just to watch?" I ask hopefully.

My dad considers for a second. He already said he has the afternoon free. It's hard to walk that back now.

"If it means that much to you. All right. Let's do it."

20

AN ABSOLUTE MISSILE

I thought people at Oakwood were excited for the spring dance, but Monday morning changes my mind.

They're not excited.

They're obsessed.

I swear, dance mania has reached crisis levels. In all my classes, it's: *Where are you going to dinner? What're you wearing? Did you hear what so-and-so said to so-and-so?*

Nobody seems to be talking about Griffin—and nobody's bothering me either way—so I guess that means Luca kept his word.

Maybe going as fifth wheel in their group wouldn't be so bad. I do like Julie, and Ashley seems pretty cool, too.

I wonder what Griffin's planning. If he's still working on his waltz and tango.

When I get to lunch, Henry and Amit are already there, deep in conversation about the game against B-Prep.

"Glad to see you back," Amit tells me. "Sorry you're still not feeling well."

I guess he doesn't know I was at school on Friday, alone in the library.

"I actually have some good news on that front," I say.

"Oh, yeah?" Henry asks.

"After you left my house yesterday, my dad changed his mind and said I could come watch tomorrow's game."

"Sweet," Amit says.

"That's awesome," Henry agrees. "And that's okay with your doctor?"

"We didn't ask. It really was more my dad saying I couldn't go in the first place."

"Well, all right then," Henry says.

That's when Luca sits down, looking like an active volcano. He rips open his brown bag lunch and takes the angriest bite of apple I've ever seen. Amit catches my eye. I can tell he's trying not to laugh.

"Something funny?" Luca snarls.

"Whoa, chill out, dude," Henry says. "You want to tell us what happened?"

"Nope."

"Come on. We're your team. Is this about Ashley?"

Luca doesn't say anything. Just opens his bag of chips and eats a whole handful at once.

"That bad, huh?" Henry asks.

"She said she's already going with Marvin Yu. The guy on the track team."

"Aw, man, I'm sorry. I didn't know." Henry offers Luca a consoling pat on the back.

"Yeah, well, that's what I get for waiting. No way would she have said yes to Marvin if I'd gotten there first."

Amit catches my eye again. It's funny—for a man of few words, he can certainly communicate a lot. Maybe it's a takes-one-to-know-one situation.

"You want to say something, Will?" Luca asks bitterly.

"What? No. Just—sorry, dude. That sucks."

Luca huffs, like he's doing his best big bad wolf.

"Who are you planning to ask, by the way? You know the dance is this Friday."

"Me? Oh, I—I wasn't planning to ask anybody," I stammer. "I'm still not sure if I'm going."

"Not *going*? The whole *school's* going. Is this another disease thing, or are you just scared of all the girls who will be there?"

He says it like it's funny. Like it means nothing at all.

"I just don't really feel like it," I manage to get out.

Henry shoots daggers at Luca with his eyes. Amit pretends not to notice, but it's obvious there's more going on underneath Luca's words. Sometimes I think that's why he acts the way he does. He wants you to believe he knows something you don't. He wants you to think that there are secrets everywhere, and he's in on all of them.

"We were just talking about our strategy for B-Prep before you got here," Henry says. Translation: cut it out, Luca.

Luca doesn't seem ready to cut it out, but whatever else he's about to say, he thinks better of it at the last second. To Henry, he says, "Oh yeah?"

"Yeah. You remember from the regular season how their offense is really strong, but their goalie's the mayor of Awful-town? Well, I say we plan to just keep hammering at their goal as often as possible. Bring our defense forward and just *bam, bam, bam.*"

Something flickers across Luca's face at the mention of their goalie. Like he feels the pressure. A hundred dollars says he's picturing the B-Prep guys having the exact same conversation at their lunch table about him.

If it were anyone else, I might actually feel sorry for him. But I'm really getting tired of Luca's whole deal. And the funny thing about having other friends is, I don't feel like I have to work so hard to keep the peace. Life's too short.

"Sounds like a solid plan," I say. "Not much you can do when your goalie's off his game."

"What's that supposed to mean?" Luca says.

I shrug innocently.

"At least I'm playing in the game."

"Guys," Henry says. "Seriously. I feel like I'm babysitting here."

It's a staring contest, and neither Luca nor I back down.

If he thinks I'm going to be the first one to break and apologize, he can think again.

I can play this game until I'm blue in the face.

I feel untouchable when I show up to school on Tuesday wearing my travel jersey. Dad talked to Coach Yosef and

Principal Baylor, and they both agreed I could wear it and leave early, when the team does. The only conditions were that I had to tell my dad if I started feeling sick, and I had to catch up on all my missing and late assignments last night. I guess Principal Baylor told my dad that my teachers were worried about me.

I stayed up till almost midnight, but I got everything done.

Walking down the hall to first period, I realize how much I've missed this feeling. It might not hold up in a Mirror Realms battle, but this travel jersey is its own kind of armor. It tells everyone else I have a whole team behind me, and I swear people look at me differently when I'm wearing it. Even teachers.

I can barely sit still through my morning classes.

It's not just excitement for the game, either. As much as I can't wait for the look on Henry's face when he sees me in my jersey, I know I'll get that chance at the game. When the bell rings for lunch, I decide I'm not going to let Luca's attitude ruin this rare good day, and I head to the library instead.

Griffin's standing right outside the door when I get there, scarfing down a sandwich he brought from home.

"Erm mah gorm, Wer," he says around a mouthful of food, covering his face with his hand so he can finish his bite in peace. Then he says, "Didn't expect to see you."

"I didn't really feel like going to the cafeteria. Okay if I join you?"

"Sure," he says, but he sounds a little suspicious. I guess I can't blame him, after what happened last time. "But are you not going to eat?"

"Oh, uh, I already ate," I say. The truth is, I came up with a plan to avoid getting sick at the game this afternoon. Instead of eating my full lunch, I'm planning to eat just my bag of saltine crackers, and I'm going to do it in my dad's car on the way to the game. Hopefully, if my stomach's already empty, there won't be any more emptying to do.

"Okay, well, let me just finish this right quick." He puts the rest of the sandwich in his mouth. As soon as he starts chewing, he notices my travel jersey. "Aroo pwaying?" he asks excitedly, barely getting his hand up to cover his mouth in time.

"Nah," I say. "Just going to watch."

"Ah. Still cool."

I follow Griffin in, over to the bank of computers. I

catch Ms. Steinem's eye on the way, and give her a look that I hope says, *See? I'm not totally evil.*

"So did you want to play Mirror Realms, or what?" Griffin asks.

"Yeah, that sounds good."

"We really can't go on a quest, though. Library rules. Building realms only."

"No worries."

We log in and choose the option to teleport to a building realm, where individual users and their friends can go and make all kinds of structures, limited only by what's in their inventories. Griffin shows me the houseboat he's been working on, which doesn't look that big, to be honest, but which he says has taken him three months of dedicated building already. Every time he finds a new detail to describe, he gets excited, but then it's like he catches himself and slows back down. He keeps shooting me looks out of the corner of his eye, like he's checking to make sure I'm not bored.

"This is one awesome houseboat," I say.

"Right?"

"It would be so cool if you had this in real life. You could go anywhere, and you'd have everything you need."

"Exactly," Griffin says. "Exactly."

I can feel my heartbeat speeding up a little bit. Even though there's no one else in here. Even though it's just Griffin and me.

"Hey, um," I start, before I can change my mind. "What do you think you're doing for the dance? I mean, are you still doing those classes?"

"Oh," Griffin says. "I decided I'm not going. To the spring dance, I mean. My mom already paid for the classes, so . . ."

"Oh, okay. Yeah. I was thinking I'm probably not going to go either. Like, why's it such a big deal, right? It's not even going to be any fun."

"Yeah," Griffin says. "My thing is, I just don't really feel welcome at this school. Like that guy, Luca? I'm sorry, I know he's your friend, but he's actually just mean. And he's not the only one here. Do you know how many people still come up to me a year after *The Wizard of Oz* and ask what does a gay lion roar sound like? I know that's why Mr. Ibsen made me stage manager this year, no matter what he says about spreading the experience around."

My chest is tight. I feel like I can't breathe. It's so not

fair that people are treating Griffin like that. Even if I thought it might be happening—even if it's what I was afraid of, all along—hearing it confirmed is like a punch to the gut.

"I'm so sorry," I hear myself say. They're the same words people keep saying to me when they find out I have Crohn's disease. I wish I had better words to tell Griffin everything I'm feeling right now.

"Well, it's not your fault," Griffin says. "Honestly, I blame the school. Do you know how easy it would be for our school to start a Genders and Sexualities Alliance? Or to include LGBTQ people in the no-discrimination policy? Heck, I'd even settle for safe space posters."

My heartbeat is full-on racing now. He isn't outright saying if he identifies with one of those letters himself. And maybe it would be wrong to press. Maybe I'd be just like the people who ask him to do a gay lion voice. Maybe I'm supposed to let him tell me whatever he feels comfortable telling me.

"Sounds like you've given this some thought," I manage.

"A lot of the schools in Atlanta have this stuff. I hear about it when I go to my theater classes. I wish my mom would move us somewhere else, but she says there's no way she could afford to open a bakery in Atlanta." Griffin sighs. "So yeah, no dance for me."

However Griffin identifies, this is the second time he's said he'd have to leave Oakwood to feel like he belongs. It's like Francis Redmond all over again. It's not okay.

But now I know one thing. He's talked to his mom about this. He's strategized with people in his theater classes.

Griffin is every bit as brave as I imagined he'd be last year. And I'm starting to feel like I need to be brave, too, even if I still have that spinning-out-race-car feeling at the same time. Maybe they can coexist.

I say, "For what it's worth, I thought you made an awesome Cowardly Lion."

Finally, the end of fifth period rolls around, and the announcement comes on calling all soccer players to the bus loading zone. Rashawn, Kent, and I all proudly gather our stuff to leave as Mr. Hayward wishes us luck. Someone in the class even starts up a chant: *Acorns. Acorns.*

When we reach the loading zone, my dad's SUV is pulled up right behind the bus. I don't even care when the guys have to get in line for the bus without me. Henry gives me two thumbs-up and a holler when he sees my jersey. I climb into my dad's passenger seat with the biggest smile on my face.

"How you feeling today, champ?"

"Pretty good," I say. Because right now, it's true.

"How many trips to the bathroom so far?"

"Just a few," I say, which is also true. Even before my talk with Griffin in the library, my stomach felt a little jittery all day. How could it not, with such a big, important game on the line? I'm as nervous for us to win as I am about getting sick.

At least since I'm riding with my dad, we can stop if I really have to go to the bathroom between here and the game. And apparently, there are nice bathrooms just a short walk away from the visitor bleachers. Dad called them yesterday to check. (I guess it's a private school thing.)

Still, to be on the safe side, I decide I'd better go ahead and *not* eat the crackers I'd saved for the car ride. I'm hungry enough that my stomach is making some pretty weird noises, but with my nerves all over the place, I just don't think it's worth the risk.

"A few?" my dad asks, like this is a lot.

"A couple," I say, although I guess it was more than two. I at least tried not to go twice in any one class, so my teachers wouldn't worry too much.

"Hmm. You remember the deal, right? You'll tell me if you're not feeling well?"

"Yes, I remember," I say. "Can we listen to music?"

"Is the sky blue?" Dad says, setting the station to country and cranking the volume up. With that, we're on our way.

Compared to our dinky field and bleachers, the B-Prep soccer complex looks like it's major league material.

There aren't many Oakwood fans on our side of the field, but a few of the other parents are here, and they give Dad and me friendly waves, asking how I'm doing and if I'll be back out there myself soon. I'm relieved when we all settle in to watch the game, and I can stop answering questions.

On the field, it's all business. Henry and Kent brusquely shake hands with the B-Prep captains in the center circle, and then the game gets off to a lightning-fast start.

Just like Henry drew it up, the Acorns do everything in their power to keep the ball near the B-Prep goal. Our defenders even make a few totally reckless passes just to get the ball into enemy territory, where the Acorn offense can try to make hay with it.

It's easy to see how B-Prep made it this far into the tournament. Their offense is more coordinated than my mom's craft closet, and their defense is no slouch, either.

At defensive midfielder, Francis Redmond plays like he's possessed. Every time he and an Acorn clash over the ball, he comes out ahead. I don't know if Amit is nervous or what, but Francis is making him look like he belongs back in the Pee Wee leagues.

Unlike in our regular season game, he's wearing his rainbow socks today. I don't need to be on the sidelines to know what some of the Acorns are saying about that. But Francis's performance out there speaks for itself.

I do see why Henry singled out B-Prep's goalie, though. Where Francis is out for vengeance, their goalie seems like he is out to lunch, moving around wildly even when the ball is nowhere near him. He's got to be wasting tons of energy that way, and it's not making him any more prepared for when a shot is actually taken.

By the end of the first quarter, the score is still tied zero all, but only because Francis and the rest of the B-Prep defense kept our guys from getting anywhere close to that goalie.

Henry is trying to keep the rest of the team fired up, but it's definitely a tall order—B-Prep is *bringing it*. Even though he got schooled in the first quarter, out of everyone, Amit seems to be picking up what Henry's putting down. Luca, meanwhile, is hardly paying attention. He keeps looking over his shoulder, finding Francis with his eyes, and scowling. It's so obvious that at one point, even his dad, sitting on the far end of the bleachers, yells at him to keep his head in the game.

Henry's cheerleading pays off when the second quarter starts. Amit passes back to Rashawn, who passes all the way up to Henry, who fakes out two B-Prep defenders, smooth as ice. He breaks away and makes a charge at the goal, with Kent not far behind for the assist if he needs it. But I and everyone else in the Oakwood stands can feel it—Henry is on a breakaway tear. He's going to take a shot.

Francis and the B-Prep defenders scramble to try to

catch him and narrow the angle, but they're too late. Henry pulls back and fires off an absolute missile, and the B-Prep goalie makes a dive in the exact same instant, knowing that the only way he can stop Henry's shot in time is if he makes a guess as to where it'll go.

Unfortunately for him, he makes the wrong guess.

We erupt in cheers. Dad gives me a high five, while on the field, all the Acorns surround Henry in celebration. But only for a moment, since too much gloating over one goal would be bad sportsmanship.

To their credit, the B-Prep guys shake it off, and Francis joins a few of his teammates as they stop by their goalie to make sure he's okay. I have to give that goalie some respect. He jumped right back to his feet, and even though he looks a little bummed, he doesn't waste any time getting into position for the kickoff. He's not the mayor of Awful-town. He's trying his best.

That should be me, I think. I should be brushing myself off and getting back out there. Showing the team I'm not a quitter. That I'm more than my disease.

As if I needed a reminder of why I'm not on the field, though—why I'm stuck in the bleachers—I feel a painful churning in my stomach.

How could this be happening? I haven't eaten since breakfast.

Ow. It's like the hunger and the stomach pains are mixing together. Like a chemical reaction where the product is doom.

I hate to miss even a second of the game, but it is what it is.

"I'll be right back," I tell Dad, and he tries to hide his worry as he gives me a salute and I head to the restroom building. Let's hope it's as nice as they promised.

Remember how I said I would spare you the full details of what it's like to go to the bathroom with Crohn's disease?

That was for your benefit and mine. Like I said, it makes me feel gross to have a body that does such gross things. And it might make you feel gross to know about it, too. Without even meaning to, you'd look at me different.

But I guess I lied. Because what you have to know is, sometimes when you go to the bathroom with Crohn's disease, there's blood. That's because there are bleeding ulcers on the inside of your digestive tract, and the blood has to go somewhere. Ulcers are like little cuts.

It isn't pretty, but that's the truth.

I'm sorry.

I wish I had better words.

Sometimes, it's a lot of blood.

Like, a scary amount.

I'm not sure how long it's been when I head back to the bleachers, but it's been long enough that Dad is no longer at his seat. It's like the escape room all over again. Dad's pacing beside the bleachers, his eyes trained in my direction, like he's been waiting anxiously.

"What'd I miss?" I ask. "What's the score?"

"It's tied at one all," he says. "How are you feeling?"

"Okay," I say.

"Yeah?" he says.

"Yeah."

"Because you don't look so hot."

"Gee, thanks," I say, trying to play it off like I've got

jokes. But the truth is, I *don't* feel so hot. I feel a little clammy. There's sweat on my forehead, but I'm cold, when I wasn't before. When I try to take a step toward the bleachers, I wobble a little bit.

Dad sees it right away.

"Hey, whoa," he says. "Do we need to leave?"

"No, no," I say. "I just need to sit down."

Then I take another step, and the dizziness catches up with me.

Maybe it was a mistake to skip lunch.

Maybe . . .

I close my eyes for just a second—I swear, it feels like it's only for a second—but the next thing I know, I'm on the grass, and my dad is leaning down to scoop me up, like I'm a baby, only he's moving really fast—like, scary fast—and some of the other Oakwood parents are shouting out things like "Oh my word!" and "Is Will okay?"

I even think I hear a referee whistle from somewhere on the field.

I can't pay too much attention to that, though, because every time I blink, it's like my eyes are a little heavier, and I don't even have the energy to tell my dad to put me down.

He's on the phone, holding it between his ear and his shoulder. He tells someone, "Yes, I'll hold, but it might be an emergency."

I have just enough sense left to know he's right.

21

TYPE O-POSITIVE

I have no idea how long we're in the car. It could be five minutes, or it could be thirty. I'm too out of it to pay much attention.

All I know is, my stomach *hurts*.

At some point, Dad asks me if I ate something from the list of dangerous foods, and I tell him no—I barely ate anything today.

That only kicks him into higher gear. He actually hits the gas pedal so hard it makes a revving sound, just like in the movies. Two blocks from the hospital, he sees a green light turning yellow and absolutely floors it. That's how serious this is. Mr. Safety here is suddenly the Fast and the Furious.

Ow.

It even hurts to laugh.

Dad pulls into the parking lot of our city hospital. We don't drive by here very often, because it's on the other side of town from where we live. I guess if I had to pick a place to have an emergency, I'm glad it was at B-Prep. They're a whole lot closer.

And it *is* an emergency.

I know because Dad picks me up out of the car and walks me in through an entrance that says EMERGENCY above the sliding doors, in red block letters.

My dad starts walking toward the front desk, but a man in scrubs steps out from behind it and comes up to us right away, unfolding a wheelchair that Dad places me in. I'm too tired to protest that I can walk on my own. I'm almost too tired to keep my eyes open.

"My son has Crohn's disease. He passed out at a soccer game. He hasn't had much to eat today."

"Okay, if you could just sign your son in at that kiosk over there, I'll be right back with a nurse."

He directs Dad to a row of touchscreen computers nearby, and Dad races to fill out everything with shaking fingers. As soon as he's back at my side, he sends a few rapid-fire text messages, I'm guessing to Mom. He already talked to her in the car, and he promised to keep her updated, so she knows where to go when she gets here.

"Almost there, bud," he says, patting my shoulder. "Just stay awake for me, okay? And try to breathe."

He takes a deep breath, like he's showing me how.

The man from the desk returns with a little plastic bracelet that has my name and birthday on it.

"Is this all correct?" he asks my dad.

"Will McKeachie. August ninth. Yup, that's right."

The man puts the bracelet on my wrist and goes back to his desk. In no time, a nurse comes out and offers me a sympathetic smile, checking my new bracelet to confirm she's got the right guy. "Hi, Will. I'm Terri. We're just going to wheel you into this room right here and take your vitals, okay?"

I nod. My dad shoots up out of his chair like a rocket to follow behind us. Nurse Terri parks my wheelchair in a small exam room.

"It sounds like you fainted, is that right? And I see here you have Crohn's disease, taking prednisone and Asacol?"

I look to Dad to confirm, because I almost never say

the name of the other medicine I take besides prednisone. It's just the red pills.

He nods.

"Are you in pain?"

"Yeah," I say, motioning to my stomach.

"How bad is your pain, on a scale of one to ten?"

My dad looks at me like he needs to know, too. This is starting to feel like the worst test of my life.

"Uh . . . I don't know. Like a six or seven?"

"A six or seven," Nurse Terri repeats. Her voice is calm, but she moves lightning-fast, placing a little device on the tip of my finger, pulling down a thermometer gun to take my temperature on my forehead. "A hundred and one," she says, reading the number on the screen. "So you've got a fever." Around my upper arm, she wraps a plastic-and-Velcro sleeve that inflates with air, then pulses slowly. She takes it back off with a rapid *rrrrrrriiiip*.

"Has there been any blood when you go to the bathroom?"

"Yes."

"Bright red or dark?"

"Dark."

Dad winces at that, as if it's painful for him, too. I

can't help thinking I've let him down. The deal was I'd tell him if I was feeling bad. I guess my body told him what my brain didn't want to.

"And have you been able to keep any liquids down?"

"Just a little water in the car."

"Okay, Will. I'm going to wheel you back to a bed, hook you up to an IV, and then a doctor will be with you shortly."

Dad never leaves my side, even as he keeps firing off text messages, sharing the play-by-play.

The nurse wheels me into a hospital room, which is not really a room so much as a bed surrounded on two sides by curtains. There's a solid wall in the back, and in the front, the room opens out onto a crowded hall where doctors and nurses hurry in every direction, the sound of constant beeping mixed in with their low conversations.

Nurse Terri helps my dad get me up onto the bed. She examines both my arms at the elbow, then sticks my right arm with a needle attached to a little syringe. It's all so fast I hardly feel a pinch. First she draws a few vials of blood for testing, and then she wheels in an IV stand with a bag that she calls a saline drip. This is supposed to help me rehydrate.

"You're doing great, Will," she says with a small smile,

and then she joins the stream of hospital staff, off to fetch the doctor.

I close my eyes and breathe.

Beep, beep, beep.

"Your mom'll be here soon," Dad assures me. He keeps taking a seat in the small chair beside my bed, then standing up again. Rinse and repeat. "Sounds like she got stuck in some rush-hour traffic. I wonder if she should bring us some dinner. I know you can't eat right now, but we could be here for a while. I'm not sure if there's enough room for both of us in here. We might have to take turns."

"Dad," I croak, my voice dry and raspy.

"Right. Sorry. I'm babbling. I know." He leans in so he can say the next part more quietly. "Hospitals just give me the heebie-jeebies, if I'm being honest. That's probably not a very adult thing to say right now."

"I don't mind. It's real."

"You're going to be okay, Will. I have every faith."

It turns out I'm not just low on fluids. The test results showed that my hemoglobin count is below the healthy range, which is doctor-speak for I've lost a lot of blood.

That's according to Dr. Chen. He seems nice enough for

a male doctor. When he first came in with Nurse Terri, he smiled and said he was going to take care of me. But he's not Dr. Clarkson, which is sort of freaking me out. She was my Crohn's coach, and now she's not here. It's like I got traded to another team in the middle of the season, without any of the perks.

Dr. Chen says they're going to need some pictures of my stomach using what's called a CT scan, and then later they'll have to give me either a blood transfusion or an iron infusion to replace what I've lost.

If it hadn't hit me how serious this was before, the phrase "blood transfusion" makes it sink in now. I might literally need someone else's blood pumped into me, like Frankenstein's monster.

Hearing the news, Dad looks like he wants to take a turn with the whole fainting thing, but luckily Mom shows up to provide reinforcements.

She doesn't say anything when she comes in my little curtained-off space. She just takes the room in one big step, then hugs the bejeezus out of the top of my head, careful not to touch the tubes and needles poking out of me. She holds on to me for a solid minute, and I don't even mind. I'm too happy to have her here.

It turns out I have blood type O-positive. Dr. Chen says that's good news, because it's the most common blood type, and if I do have to get a blood transfusion, it shouldn't take long to prepare.

After all the things that have gone wrong today, I guess it's nice to know there is *something* common about me.

Before the blood transfusion, Dr. Chen wants me to be admitted to the hospital. I thought I already *was* admitted, but come to find out, when you first get to the ER, you're considered "outpatient," which I imagine means I could still run out at any minute.

And I kind of do want to run out, hearing all this news.

Dad says not to worry. That Dr. Chen just wants the hospital doctors to keep an eye on me overnight. To be on the safe side.

I know that's not the full story, though. I heard Dr. Chen tell my parents in the hallway that I might have to be in here for a few days.

Beep beep beep.

I'm still too tired to worry much about what comes next.

I wish I could go to sleep and wake up when it's all over.

* * *

The CT scan is a little weird, but okay. First, they make me lie on a table sticking out of this giant tube that looks like something you'd see on a spaceship. Then they put this liquid into my IV that makes me feel warm all over before it makes me feel like I have to pee. That's the weirdest part.

The table I'm lying on slides into the tube. I've never been in a tanning bed, but this is what I've always imagined they're like.

And then that part's done. Way easier than my colonoscopy was.

Looking at the results, Dr. Chen says it's good news: there aren't any signs of major blockages in my intestines. If there had been, I might have needed surgery to remove the blocked parts, so for now, we're all breathing a sigh of relief.

Still, between the fact that I'm still bleeding every time I go to the bathroom and the fact that I'm still running a fever, with pain in my stomach, I'm not out of the woods yet.

So it's back in the wheelchair and up to my new hospital room.

You know, it's funny.

My phone died almost as soon as they brought me back here. I guess between makeup work and pregame jitters, I forgot to charge it last night. But all this time without my phone to distract me, it's not the B-Prep game or the spring dance that's on my mind as they wheel me from one place to the next.

Nope.

I keep thinking about our church's sanctuary, and not just the sanctuary—that stained-glass window.

Is that how my body will be, after this is all over? Fixed, but only sort of—the blue pane of glass in a sea of bluish green?

It turns out being admitted to the hospital also means an all-new doctor and all-new nurses. I swear, this place has more rules than school.

But Dr. Rubenstein says she knows Dr. Clarkson from "way back," and that she's already put a call in to her, so they can compare notes. In the meantime, they're giving me another corticosteroid. Not a pill, like prednisone. This one is through my IV. She looked at all my test results, and she's hopeful that after this, an iron infusion will be enough, without my needing new blood. That won't happen until tomorrow either way. Tonight, there's a lot of waiting around.

At least this new room is an actual room, with four walls and windows and a reclining chair beside my bed.

Mom and Dad keep taking turns in that chair, while the other steps out into the hall, sometimes to talk on the phone, sometimes to make a trip down to the vending machines. Lexie isn't coming tonight because it's after visiting hours. But over my mom's phone, she says, "I love you. You're strong." She doesn't even make a single joke.

My parents don't say it, but the shifts are partly because when all three of us are in the room, the energy becomes too antsy. Too full. We need each other, but we also need some space.

Around nine o'clock, Dad waves his phone at me.

"I just heard from Mark," he says. Mark is Henry's dad. "The team is all sending good vibes."

"How much did they see?" Without my phone, I haven't had a chance to talk to anyone. Not that I'm much in the mood for talking anyway.

"Enough that they know you can use all the good vibes you can get," Dad says.

In normal times, this news would be humiliating. I

try so hard to keep attention away from myself, only to have my whole team and the whole B-Prep team see me faint on the sidelines.

But for some reason, the news just washes over me. It's like the embarrassment is balanced out by the fact that everybody knows the truth now. I don't have to pretend to be okay anymore, because they all know I'm not.

"Do you want to know what happened in the game?" Dad says. "Or is it too soon?"

"You can tell me," I say.

"It came down to a shootout in overtime, and Brookside just barely eked out the win by one."

"Wow."

Poor Luca. After all that talk about B-Prep's goalie being the weak link, I can't believe it came down to a shootout, the most high-pressure situation for any goalie. I feel sort of bad for adding to that pressure at lunch yesterday. Luca is probably beating himself up.

Luca has not been a good friend for a while now, but that doesn't mean I had to be a bad friend, too.

"Dad?"

"Yeah, bud?"

"I think I do want to talk to Dr. Gregory this week."

Dad suddenly looks panicked.

"You know you're going to be fine, Will," he says. "Once you've got this blood or this iron in you, your doctors are going to figure out a different set of medicines to take so it doesn't get this bad again."

"That's good," I say. "But I still want to talk to him. I have a question I've been wondering about."

Dad lets out a sigh, a little less worried now that he knows I don't think I'm on my death bed or something.

"We'll make sure you get a chance to talk to him," he says. Then, so quietly I can barely hear him, he adds, "Maybe I'll talk to him, too."

"Dad?"

"Yeah, bud?"

"I'm really glad you were at the game with me."

My dad reaches out to hold my hand, but he doesn't say anything. Or at least, I don't think he does. The next thing I know, I'm fast asleep.

22

WELL WISHES

The sun shines through my hospital window, and I wake up feeling alive, which is more than I can say for yesterday, now that I think about it.

My mom's asleep in the reclining chair, a thin, blue blanket barely covering her legs. She must've gone home at some point, though, because she's wearing a different shirt. And someone—probably Mom—plugged my phone into a charger. It's sitting on my bedside table, the screen lit up with notifications.

There's a flood of texts from Henry asking if I'm okay. There are messages from some of the other Weekend Warriors, too, including Yasmin and Madison. There's even a message from Griffin, who says he heard from

Julie, who must've talked to Henry.

I guess word travels fast.

I can't help noticing there are no messages from Luca. I'm sure he's still mad about picking up that second loss, but it's hard not to feel a little hurt, to be honest.

I take a selfie in my hospital bed—a picture of a boy amid all these tubes and wires. I text it to Griffin, Henry, Yasmin, and Madison, with a message that says, Not 100%, but feeling better today.

I don't expect to get many messages back, since it's a school day and everyone is probably already in first period. But I guess everyone else is better at hiding their phone under their desk than I am, because the responses start coming in right away.

Griffin's response makes me laugh so loud it finally wakes up my mom.

Maybe some of the monsters you healed can return the favor? it says. But srsly, hang in there.

Dr. Rubenstein seems pleased when she comes to check on me.

"Your fever's down, and you look like you have a little more energy. How are you feeling?"

"Better," I say.

"You should've heard him laughing earlier. It woke me right up," Mom chimes in.

"Fabulous," the doctor replies. "Better is good. Now I talked to Dr. Clarkson, and she agreed that we should start you with an iron infusion and go from there. How does that sound?"

I look to my mom to answer, but she's looking to me.

"What do you think, sweetie?" she asks. "Do you have any questions?"

"I don't think so. I guess . . . is it iron, like, the metal?"

"You're exactly right," Dr. Rubenstein says. "Iron is a metal that occurs naturally in our diet. It helps our body make more blood. That's why we prefer to start there when we can. Our body's more likely to tolerate our own blood than someone else's."

"That makes sense, I think. Yeah, let's do that."

"Excellent. A nurse will be in to start the drip soon, and we'll keep monitoring you to make sure you have no bad reactions."

My mom waits until Dr. Rubenstein's out of the room to squeeze my hand.

✳ ✳ ✳

Dad arrives around lunchtime, shortly after the infusion is done. I'm flushed and a little lightheaded but mostly okay. The nurse who kept checking on me said these feelings are normal.

"How you feeling today, champ?"

I give him a thumbs-up.

"Do you think you're up for a visitor?"

I'm confused at first, thinking he means himself. Then I realize he's blocking the door and hanging on my answer.

"Oh, yeah, sure."

"In that case, look who I found out in the hallway." When he steps aside with a big cheesy flourish, Dr. Gregory is behind him, looking amused by the introduction.

"Hi there, Will."

Dr. Gregory offers me a warm smile. He's not wearing his black pastor robe that he wears on Sundays. Instead, he's in khakis and a button-up shirt, with a pen sticking out of his shirt pocket. Somehow, the wardrobe change makes him much less intimidating than he is in church. Still, I can't believe my dad brought him here *today*, when I'm stuck in a hospital bed, wearing one of these horrible gowns. I guess I did say I wanted to talk to him, but I meant, like, after. When I could get back to church.

Mom stands up to greet him.

"Thank you so much for coming," she says.

"I'm happy to be here. Will, I've heard you're having quite the week."

"It's a doozy," I agree.

"A doozy. That's right." Dr. Gregory smiles. "Well, your mom and dad invited me to come pay a visit, and I'm so glad they did, because I'm here with the well wishes of a whole congregation that has been praying hard for you these past few weeks."

I'm not sure what to say to that.

"Thanks," I manage.

"We'll just head down to the cafeteria to get some lunch," Dad says. "But we'll be right back."

"Don't eat anything too good," I joke, gesturing to the IV bag that is providing all my meals.

"Don't worry, we won't."

And then they're gone, and Dr. Gregory sits in the chair beside my bed.

"That's a nice window view you have," Dr. Gregory says. "Some of the rooms in here are cut off from the outside, and I always find it concerning. I think the natural light helps with healing."

"Do you have to visit people here a lot?"

"Oh, a fair bit," Dr. Gregory says. "It comes with the pastor territory. But I get to hold a lot of babies, too, so it all balances out."

"I heard my dad talks to you. For spiritual guidance."

"Your dad's a good man," Dr. Gregory says. "He cares about you a lot."

"I can tell it bums him out that I haven't been playing soccer in a while."

"I think what bums him out is that you're not feeling well."

"Yeah. It bums me out too."

"You know, Will, I'm happy to offer what support I can, but there are some real benefits to seeing a licensed counselor, when you're going through something as big as what you're going through. It's easy to sweep all the mental stuff under the rug when you're busy with the physical stuff, but there are doctors for both for a reason."

"*Another* doctor?" I say, like I'm saying something funny, but Dr. Gregory gives me a smile that somehow lets me know he's being serious at the same time.

"It's just kind of embarrassing," I say.

"What is?"

"All of it. Having to tell all these doctors about going to the bathroom and stuff. The thought of having to tell even more doctors about . . . mental stuff . . . It makes me feel . . . weak, I guess."

"I know it's hard, Will, but I also know that needing help is not a sign of weakness. In fact, knowing when to ask for help is a sign of strength. Do you know, one of my favorite things about a church is that it's a whole community of people who can help one another in times of need? That's what we're all called to do. That's *our* strength."

"My science teacher said something like that the other day. That I should ask for help more."

"Sounds like a good teacher to me."

"She mostly is. She gives a lot of homework."

Dr. Gregory laughs.

"I have to be honest with you," he says. "I don't miss those days."

It's a lot easier to talk to Dr. Gregory than I thought it would be. I guess I can see why my mom suggested it in the first place.

"Dr. Gregory, can I ask you something?"

"Of course," he says.

"In Weekend Warriors the other day, Mr. Dyson read us a passage from First Corinthians about bad company. Do you know it?"

"I do indeed," Dr. Gregory says. "I remember teaching it to my own Sunday school students many years ago. It's a good lesson when you're at that age when peer pressure starts to become a more serious issue."

"Well, then our class got into a discussion about whether a girl who has two moms is bad company or not. Because of her moms."

"I heard about that," Dr. Gregory says. He leans forward in the chair, propping his elbows on his knees. "Eric— Mr. Dyson—came to talk to me that day. Sounds like he tried to make it clear that not being unduly influenced by others does not mean it's open season to judge others."

"Right," I say. "He did make that clear. I think."

"Good."

"But I'm still a little confused about what it means for that girl and her moms. Would they be welcome in our church?"

"Aha," Dr. Gregory says. "I see. You know, Will, the fact that you're not sure makes me feel like I've already

254

dropped the ball a bit as your pastor."

I wait for him to go on. I can feel my heart thumping in my chest, and I don't think it's from the iron.

"The first thing I want to say is that a church is like a school. I try to set an example through my sermons, and through my Bible study teachers, the same way your principal does with staff meetings and morning announcements. But churches and schools are full of individuals who will make their own choices and have their own beliefs. One thing I prize about our church, specifically, is that we encourage that individuality."

"So you're saying some people would welcome them, and some people wouldn't?"

"Well, that's where it gets a little complicated," Dr. Gregory says, and it's clear he really means it. He's not just trying to dumb something down because I'm in middle school. "My *hope* is that the church would welcome this girl and her moms."

"But?"

"But, well . . . We have some very, ah, *traditional* Baptists at our church who may not be as open to the *idea* of two moms as I would hope. I'd like to think, though, that if this family were to come to our church, our parishioners would follow the example set by myself and my Sunday school teachers and treat them with respect."

I think about what Griffin said about how our school could be more welcoming if it had a clear policy. I try to muster up some of his courage.

"I just don't know if this family would come to our church, unless they knew they were welcome first. Does our church have something on our website that includes LGBTQ people?"

Dr. Gregory leans back in his chair and considers this.

"You know, Will, we don't. But I see your point. Maybe we could have a clearer mission statement when it comes to inclusion."

"That could be good," I say.

"See, this is why I enjoy talking to young people," Dr. Gregory says. "Sometimes we adults get so locked in our ways, we need the young people to remind us what needs changing. When your parents told me you had a question for me, I said, well, I definitely want to hear it."

"Oh. That actually wasn't the question," I say.

"No?"

I shake my head. "I didn't mean to make you come all the way up to the hospital for this, but I was wondering something else."

"All right then. What were you wondering?"

"Well, um, do you know that stained-glass window that had the cracks in it last year? The one in the sanctuary?"

"Ah, yes, the miracle window."

"Miracle window?" I ask.

"A divine reminder that we must face every day with a sense of humor," Dr. Gregory says. When I'm still confused, he explains, "It was already the miracle window, because it depicts Jesus using five loaves of bread to feed five thousand people. But now it's doubly the miracle window, because it's a miracle we were able to find a craftsperson who was able to fix it."

"Oh," I say.

"What did you want to ask about it?"

"Well . . . the thing is, I'm actually the one who broke it."

"Is that right?" Dr. Gregory says, his face crinkling.

"Yeah. It was an accident during the lock-in last year. I was playing with a bean bag when I shouldn't have been, and it got away from me. I was so scared it couldn't be fixed. And I was scared of getting in trouble."

"I see," Dr. Gregory says. "Well, I appreciate your telling me now. We all make mistakes, you know. Maybe you've heard the saying, 'To err is human, to forgive divine'?"

I shake my head. "Do you think . . . do you think my Crohn's disease could be like a punishment from God? For being bad?"

I see a wave of surprise pass over Dr. Gregory's face, replaced briefly by sadness, before it settles on concern.

"Oh, Will. No. No, I don't think that. Humans break things. And humans break. But God forgives us. He helps us fix things. Even if it's not the way we expected them to be fixed."

That's when my parents come back into the room.

"How's it going in here?" Dad says, almost like he's nervous to hear the answer.

"Good," I say.

"Your son was giving me some important things to think about."

"Oh yeah?" Dad says.

Dr. Gregory smiles. "He's a wise man. Not that I'm surprised, since he comes from wise parents."

Then Dr. Gregory gets to his feet, looks me in the eye,

and gives me a handshake.

"You've got a whole church praying for you, Will. Don't you forget it."

Then he and my parents say their goodbyes in the hallway. They're out there for a while, but I don't even mind if they're talking about me.

It feels good to be honest. It feels sort of like healing.

23

A SURPRISE

I'm not going to lie. It's a rough few days in the hospital.

Even though the iron infusion went smoothly, the issue is that I'm still losing blood when I go to the bathroom. Not as much as I did on Tuesday—not since they started giving me the steroids in my IV. But enough that they've kept me here all week for monitoring, and enough that they're still using the IV for nutrients. No solid foods.

Dr. Rubenstein says that since the steroids aren't a long-term solution anyway, what she and Dr. Clarkson would both like to do is treat this aggressively, starting me on a new medication as early as Friday. One more thing that will come right through the IV. I can get it at this hospital this time, but if it works, I'll have to go back up to Atlanta in two weeks for another infusion.

It's a scary word, *aggressive*. It makes me think of the cheerleaders at the high school, who every fall shout for the football team to *B. E. Aggressive!*

What they mean is it's time to ram through the opposing defense.

I'm afraid to think of a medicine ramming through my body's defenses, but Dr. Rubenstein says my Crohn's disease is making my body attack itself, so maybe this aggressive medicine will help me B. E. Defensive.

Honestly, I'm willing to try anything at this point.

My phone rings on Thursday, after the sun has gone down, and I'm surprised to see that it's Henry calling. We never talk on the phone. Only text.

"What's up?" I say, mouthing the word "Henry" to my mom when she looks up from her book.

"Will, man, how are you? You hanging in there?"

"For now. But ask me again in five minutes."

"That bad still?"

"Pretty much."

"I wanted to come visit you, but my dad says the hospital has visitor limits. And that you don't need my germs."

His dad's probably right. Because of the steroid in my IV, my immune system is weaker than normal right now. Still, a visit from Henry would've been cool.

"Hopefully I'll get to go home soon. We can hang out then."

"That's why I'm calling. I figure the answer is probably no, but I didn't want to assume. Do you think you're coming to the dance tomorrow? Julie and I are trying to figure out dinner. The invitation's still open, if you want to join."

"Thanks," I say, "but yeah. I don't think there's any way I'll be out of here in time. You guys have fun, though."

"It won't be as much fun without you."

"That's true."

"Hey now!" Henry laughs.

"I'm sorry you guys lost on Tuesday."

"Eh, it wasn't our year. Next year, though. We're going all the way to the top."

"You know, I haven't heard from Luca at all this week."

Henry goes quiet for a second.

"I think he's taking the loss a lot harder than I am," he finally says.

"Okay."

"You guys really don't get along, huh?"

The way he says it, it's clear he's not blaming or accusing me of something. It's like it's just a fact.

"We really don't," I admit. If this week has taught me anything, it's the importance of honesty. Life's too short for the other thing. "And to be honest, I don't know if I want to keep trying. Not that I want to tell you who you can be friends with. But for me, I'll see him at practices and stuff, but I think I'd rather spend the rest of my lunches this year in the library."

My mom raises an eyebrow, and I give her a look to let her know I'll explain everything in a minute.

"I guess I get it," Henry says. "And who knows, maybe if you give him time, he'll surprise you."

"Maybe."

"Feel better, okay, Will?"

"I'm trying my best."

The next morning, I'm still not back to a hundred percent, and I wake up feeling nervous about this new medicine. I want to believe so bad it will help, but I don't want to get my hopes up, either.

Today is Mom's day to take off work, and there is one

bright spot: there's a marathon of *Simon Says Danger* reruns on one of the TV stations we can get in my room. Mom said it's a sign that the rest of the day is going to go our way, too.

We're already two episodes in when Dr. Rubenstein and the nurses arrive with another IV bag. My new medicine is here.

"How are we holding up today, Will?" Dr. Rubenstein says. I've really come to appreciate this week how she says "we" when she means me, just like Dr. Clarkson. It makes it feel like we're all on the same team.

"Okay," I say.

"I'll be sticking around this morning to make sure the Remicade infusion goes smoothly. Just like with the iron, there's a very small chance you could have a reaction, so if you experience chest pain or difficulty breathing, just say the word, and we'll stop. But most patients don't experience that. I have a good feeling about this medication for you, Will."

I almost ask her if the reactions are because this medicine is made from mouse proteins—something Dad discovered when he was reading about it yesterday. But maybe it's better if I don't know. Maybe I've had enough science for one week.

"I have a good feeling, too," I say.

She smiles.

When they hook up the IV and the medicine starts going in, it's a bit like the iron. I feel this pressure around my IV, and then warm all over. The infusion is supposed to take two hours, which means Mom and I get two whole episodes of *Simon Says Danger* while Dr. Rubenstein and the nurses come in and out to check on me.

I don't show any of the signs of a bad reaction. At least not yet. There's still a chance I could have a reaction after a few days, but Dr. Rubenstein says I'm doing a great job so far, and she's very encouraged.

Amazingly, I don't have to go to the bathroom once during the whole infusion.

Dr. Rubenstein says that's encouraging, too.

Dad and Lexie surprise me by visiting soon after lunch.

"But—school?" I ask Lexie, giving her a hug like we're both made of glass.

"You're missing it, aren't you? Why should you have all the fun?"

"I have to send a few emails," Dad says, holding up the

laptop he uses for work, "but I figured I could at least be with my crew while I'm at it."

"You just really love family days, huh?" I tease.

"Enjoy the free digs while you can take 'em," Dad replies, messing up my hair.

We all end up watching *Simon Says Danger*, with Lexie and Dad sitting in small chairs they're allowed to bring in from the hall. If I get no other wins this week, I'll always have the fact that Dad and Lexie finally admit it's a good show.

"I always thought the only reason to watch this show was dreamy Detective Simon," Lexie says, "but the mystery's actually interesting. I have no idea who did it."

"And also, Detective Simon is dreamy," Mom says.

I groan.

A little after four, Dad's phone buzzes with a message that makes him scrunch up his face in confusion.

"I have to step out to make a phone call," he says, which is weird, because he's been making work calls in here all day (even when Mom and I tried to shush him so we could hear Detective Simon, who basically whispers all his lines).

"Everything okay?" Mom asks him, and he says, "What?

Oh, yeah," like he's super distracted.

He comes back about fifteen minutes later, and I swear, he's wiping his eyes, as if he's been crying. But he's smiling too, so I could be wrong. He gets back on his laptop and starts typing away, never mentioning anything more about his trip to the hall.

I almost forget about it, until around six o'clock when the marathon ends, and Dad asks Mom if she could step outside so they can talk about dinner plans.

That's when I know something is up. They've been talking about dinner plans right in front of me all week.

When they come back in, Mom now has the same happy-sad smile Dad had earlier, like she's just watched an episode of one of those life makeover shows.

"Okay, what's going on?" I ask.

"We have a surprise for you," Dad says.

"Well, we get to tell you about it," Mom says. "But it's not really our surprise to give."

"Okay?" I say. This is all very suspicious. I can tell Lexie has no idea what they're talking about.

Dad makes a few clicks on his laptop, and then he hands it over to me.

On the screen is the log-in page for Mirror Realms.

He would've had to download the game directly to have this screen pop up.

"How did you figure out how to get Mirror Realms on your laptop?" I ask.

"Mark walked me through it," he says, like that explains it.

"Mark? You mean Henry's dad?"

Dad nods.

"I don't get it."

"You will," Dad says. "Just sign on."

"Log in," I correct.

"Will!"

"I'm going, I'm going."

The three of them are all watching me expectantly. I log in, Willnot spawning in the cloud realm, right where I left him before Griffin and I went to his building realm earlier.

Right away, I hear the ping of an incoming message. It's from Griffin.

I lit a beacon for you. Come join for a surprise.

I check the map. The beacon is in the dream realm. My favorite home base. I teleport there, my brain racing to piece together what Griffin, the dream realm, and

Henry's dad all have to do with each other.

I arrive at the beacon location to find Griffin's Fighter standing beside a giant vortex of some sort. It's like a swirling mass of light surrounded by a crystal archway.

What is that? I ask.

It's a portal to a special building realm, Griffin says, like this explains everything.

Special?

You'll see, Griffin says. *All the guilds use these for their meeting halls.*

Cool, I say, still not totally getting it.

Before we go in, Griffin says, *I have some inventory you'll need.*

I get multiple pings in a row, notifying me that Griffin is gifting me some loot. The first item is an article of clothing called Formalwear. The second item is another article of clothing called Alric's Cloak, and when I read the flavor text, I learn that Alric was a legendary Healer, and his cloak contains some of his magic, stitched into the cloth. The third item is a Rosewood Staff, which doesn't appear to have any special properties at all.

Should I definitely equip the staff? I say. *It lowers my fighting stats.*

Yes, Griffin says. *Don't worry about stats. I just thought a Rosewood Staff would be cooler than a regular flower.*

With that, Griffin's Fighter walks through the portal, and I follow him, as confused as ever.

On the other side of the portal is the coolest location I have ever seen in Mirror Realms. It's like the inside of a giant castle, with stone columns that stretch all the way up to a distant ceiling. There are stained-glass windows on every wall, and statues of winged creatures that look like eagles with four legs.

Up ahead, I see a few other characters standing just in front of the steps that lead up to two giant thrones. I follow Griffin to where these characters are waiting.

I receive a flurry of pings to signal incoming messages.

Will! a giant ogre Fighter named HenrylzC00L says.

You made it! says the familiar Scholar I know to be Lady_J, as dark purple magic swirls all around her.

Hey Will! says a Healer named Ashlord5000.

The fourth character, another Scholar, doesn't say anything at first. He just keeps shooting bursts of colorful magic into the room, so that it looks like there are fireworks inside the castle. Hovering the mouse over the character, I see his name is Amitima. Amit plus Amit, reflected in a mirror.

"What is this?" I say, and it's funny, because I meant to say it in game. I'm just so caught up in the magic, I tried to use my real voice.

"We're going to give you some time with your friends," Dad says, back in the real world. "We'll just grab some dinner and be back in a bit."

I nod and give my family a thumbs-up, barely taking my eyes off the game.

What is this? I say, this time as Willnot.

It was Julie's good idea, Griffin says.

And Griffin helped, Henry says.

We were so bummed that you couldn't join us tonight, Julie says. *So we decided to bring the dance to you.*

We told the mods about your story, and they hooked us up with a castle you're only supposed to get if your guild has at least 100 members, Griffin explains. *Aren't the griffin statues sweet?*

I'm smiling, and I know I'm smiling, because I haven't smiled in days. The feeling of it is almost strange on my face. A muscle I haven't exercised in a while.

I'm just so glad something good came out of my trip to the hospital this week. Griffin was able to get a castle with griffin statues.

Please tell me you guys aren't missing the dance for me, I say.

Don't worry, I'm not, Amit says, adding a winky-face emoji. Right. Because he's a sixth grader.

Only the sit-down dinner, Henry explains. *We're getting something on the way.*

Wendy's, Julie says.

Wendy's it is, Henry agrees.

And I'm meeting Marvin at the dance, Ashley says.

Why would I go to the dance when I have all these statues? Griffin asks. *I'll be here all night.*

I don't even know what to say right now. I'm just so happy.

Let's be honest, I wasn't that excited to be an extra wheel at dinner anyway, and I wasn't particularly looking forward to standing awkwardly at the edges of the gym either. I'll take partying with Griffin (and maybe Amit? Lol) in a private castle with magical fireworks and a Rosewood Staff over that any day.

Julie figures out a way to send everybody a link to a

playlist in the chat, so that we're all listening to the same music at the same time.

Henry and Amit tell me about how the guys are already planning a training schedule for this summer, so the Acorns will be stronger than ever next year, and when I come back to the team, we'll finally be league champions.

Ashley figures out that if you go up to the stained-glass windows on the walls, you can actually change them to look like whatever you draw in this pop-up window, so she makes one a picture of all our characters. I swear it is, like, professional quality.

Julie, Griffin, and I all show off our cloudshark dance, which has Henry, Amit, and Ashley swearing they're going back to free the Cloud Prince, too.

In short, it's a party.

And I wouldn't trade it for anything.

24

THE TRUTH

"Will! Send it!" Henry calls, breaking away from Kent just in time for me to target a pass his way before Rashawn can overtake me at midfield. Henry makes a mad dash at the goal, dribbling around Amit and then sending the ball sailing into the far corner, so fast there is no way any human goalie could stop it.

But Ashley is no human goalie, as we've learned very quickly in these summer practice scrimmages. She lunges for the ball and swats it out of bounds like it's a common housefly. Kent, Rashawn, and Amit all shout and cheer.

"Snap!" Julie calls from the sidelines, where she and Griffin are hanging out on a picnic blanket Julie brought from home. They haven't been here for the full game, but they showed up a few minutes ago because we're supposed to be calling it quits soon. After this, we're all walking to get ice cream from the Scoops and Shakes where Lexie works.

A milkshake sounds so good right now. It's the middle of July in Georgia. It's basically a thousand degrees.

The best part is, Scoops and Shakes has started offering a soy version of the s'mores milkshake, especially in my honor. I still can't handle more than a little dairy without getting sick, and right now, I don't want to do anything that would reverse all the hard work we've done to heal my stomach.

Ever since the summer hit, I've been playing soccer with my friends a few times a week at the rec center field, and I haven't had to leave a game early to go to the bathroom once (knock on wood). Everybody says it's a miracle that the Remicade has worked as well as it has, and that going back to the hospital every few weeks for another infusion is small potatoes when you're talking about a miracle.

Still. I can't help praying for the day when I don't have to spend so much time inside doctors' offices. They've basically been like my second home this year. Dr. Clarkson keeps reminding us that there is no cure for Crohn's disease. Only good periods and bad periods. Remissions and flare-ups. The real work now is trying not to be so afraid of the bad periods that I miss out on the good periods. Lexie says that's something all people have to work on.

But it's hard.

After I came home from the hospital in April, I got so afraid of getting sick again that I basically only left my house for church, school, and doctors' appointments. Whenever I was home, I was playing Mirror Realms. It got to the point that I was playing a lot. Like, more than Griffin.

I don't play quite that much now.

"Is it time to go?" Julie calls.

"We're getting sunburned over here," Griffin says.

"Maybe you should've brought sunscreen," Ashley calls back, but we wrap up the game anyway, tied at three goals each, because we're all starting to feel the sun, too.

Griffin and I walk at the back of the pack all the way to Scoops and Shakes.

"Do you still have classes next week?" Griffin asks me.

I'm in summer school at the moment, after falling behind on so many classes this spring. Honestly, I was relieved when Principal Baylor suggested it. I thought I was just going to fail two classes, but by going to school in the mornings this summer, I've been able to catch up on everything I'll need for eighth grade. And I actually don't mind summer school at all. The classes are smaller, so whenever I have to give an oral report or a presentation, I don't get as nervous. I kind of wish the rest of the school year could feel like that.

"Yup," I tell Griffin. "Next week is the last week."

"Cool," he says. "Starting on Thursday, this new campaign kicks off that covers all the realms. The hunt for the red unicorn. If you find it, it gives you twenty thousand gold plus all kinds of unique items."

"Sounds awesome," I say. "How are the *Little Mermaid* rehearsals going?" Griffin didn't just get a part in the summer musical he auditioned for in Atlanta, he got *the* part—the role of Prince Eric. I already knew he was an amazing actor, but now nobody can deny it.

"Good, I think," he says. "Eric is a funny role, because I don't actually sing during any of the most famous songs from the movie. But the opener, 'Fathoms Below,' is really fun, and I even have a solo."

"I can't wait to see it."

Griffin smiles. "Yeah? You think you'll be able to come?"

"Mom said she'd take me and everything. She's excited to see it, too."

Henry runs back and stands between Griffin and me, putting his arms around both our shoulders.

"What are we talking about back here?" he says.

The Little Mermaid," I say.

"Ooookay," Henry says, kindly enough. "Back to discussing club team tryouts for me. No offense." He messes up my hair and then runs back to the front of the group. I smile. I only said *The Little Mermaid* like that because I knew it would buy Griffin and me some space.

I have to hand it to Henry. After that week in the hospital, he never tried to force me to hang out with Luca, like I thought he might. Luca and I have pretty much only talked at the end-of-year soccer banquet, and that was just a few words. Let's just say he didn't surprise me after all. According to Henry, Luca has started hanging out more with his skateboarding friends. I wonder how that's going, since it isn't a team sport. He can't blame anyone else if he misses a trick.

But that's mean, I know. I should just wish him the best.

Meanwhile, since Julie and I are both friends with

Griffin, I guess Henry decided he'd better be friends with Griffin, too. It's a little weird sometimes, but it's not a big deal.

With so many other things changing in my life, it's nice to still have Henry as a friend.

I'm especially glad that he has my back at church. Because I have to hand it to Dr. Gregory, too. It took a couple months, but after our talk in the hospital, he rallied the church to add a new inclusion policy on the website—one that says our church is expressly welcoming of families regardless of race, sexual orientation, or gender identity. He even announced it from the pulpit during a Sunday sermon. He called it "a small but important step."

For a small step, it sure made some people pretty unhappy.

Madison's dad actually made them switch churches. He said he couldn't in good faith be a deacon at a church like that. And when Mr. Dyson wasn't in the classroom one day, Zander and one of the eighth graders made this joke about how if a gay person touches you, it makes you gay. Henry shut that down. "I guess stupid's catching, too?" I swear, they just about died.

As far as I know, my family has no idea that I'm the

reason for the change. But my mom did go out of her way at dinner one night to say she thought it was a great policy. She said, "I bet there are lots of gay people already in our church, and this new statement will give them the courage to come out." Then she nudged my dad, who said he totally agreed. Lexie rolled her eyes, but she was smiling, too.

I told Griffin all about it. I said he gave me the idea to suggest the policy in the first place. He got kind of funny about that. He said he was glad my church had done the right thing, but that didn't change the fact that too many churches *aren't* safe for LGBTQ people. He's got a point. I guess I'm just glad that for once, it was the closed-minded people who had to leave, instead of the other way around.

Plus, I said that if my church could change, when so many churches won't, then maybe Oakwood could change, too.

So that's our goal for next year. One small but important step at a time.

Look, I know what you're thinking. What about *me*?

What does it mean that I feel a little bit braver every time I see Griffin? That I feel more like myself? Especially considering that Griffin is definitely the "G" in LGBTQ. He confirmed it when he asked for my help collecting twenty-five magical raindrops last month, all so he could make the rainbow "G" armor sticker during the Mirror Realms Pride event.

Am I a letter, too?

And the honest-to-goodness truth is, I'm still figuring it out. I think maybe I am gay or bi or pan, although I could be some word that doesn't exist yet. Maybe I just feel braver because Griffin lets me go with my own flow.

One thing I do know: for the first time ever, I'm not afraid to find out who I am. If people don't like me, that's on them, not me.

I see that now.

"I think I might mix it up today and try the rainbow ice cream with vanilla sprinkles," Griffin says beside me. Usually, he gets it the other way around.

"What's the occasion?" I ask.

"The occasion is it's Wednesday," Griffin says. "And I just feel happy for some reason."

"Me too," I say, and I realize I mean it.

Griffin is good company.

***

My family and I have been joking that this is the year of a thousand doctors, even if the real number is more like six or seven (I lost count a little during the emergency shuffle).

I wasn't sure how I would take to adding one more to the mix, but my parents insisted that Dr. Gregory's advice was solid, especially after Dr. Clarkson later said the same thing: I needed to see a counselor. Hence, Dr. Martinez.

Dr. Martinez has been helping me see how, just like my body attacks itself with Crohn's disease, my mind can attack itself, too, with anxiety, telling me that I'm alone when I'm really not, or that I would be a burden or embarrassment to my friends and family when I really wouldn't. She helped me see how I can't make Crohn's disease go away by pretending it isn't there. Pretending it's not there only makes it worse.

She's also helped me to see that even when I feel like things will never get better, that's just another lie my brain is telling me. Things will be bad on some days and good on some days. That's the truth.

Today, after my session with Dr. Martinez, Mom, Dad, and Lexie pick me up together. They said they have a surprise for me, to celebrate the end of summer school and a whole month of remission.

"Are we going back to the escape room?"

"No," Lexie says. "And don't try to guess. You'll ruin the surprise."

"Fine," I say. "Can we listen to music on the way?"

"We sure can," Dad says. "What station would you like?"

"Hmm . . . maybe rock?" I suggest.

"You got it," Dad says with a laugh.

So we listen to heavy metal as we drive all the way out of town, north on the interstate, headed to Atlanta. The drive is getting familiar, with all my trips to see Dr. Clarkson. But today we don't take the exit that goes to her office. We go straight past it, then take the exit at International Boulevard, and follow signs that lead to the Mercedes-Benz stadium.

"Are we going where I think we're going?" I ask.

"I said don't guess!" Lexie protests.

"Where do you think we're going?" Mom says.

"Are we going to see Atlanta United play?"

I can see my parents smiling in the rearview mirror.

It's been almost a year since we came to an Atlanta United game. With everything going on, I've barely followed the team this year.

But it turns out today is a special family day for patients at my hospital. Before the game starts, guides lead big groups of us on tours of the stadium, and a couple of the players even come out to give high fives and take selfies with us in front of the logo wall.

I look around at all the other kids and their families and I wonder what their stories are. What they're struggling with on the inside, even if I can't see it by looking at them.

I scope out the bathroom situation as we make our way to our seats, just to make sure I know where the closest ones are if I get sick during the game.

But today, I don't need them.

Today is one of the good days.

AUTHOR'S NOTE

I was diagnosed with Crohn's disease when I was in middle school, just like Will. After months of coming home exhausted from football practice and then soccer tryouts, I was relieved to have a name for what I was going through. But I was afraid of what this disease meant for my future, especially once my new medicines started to change everything from how I looked to how I felt inside.

Also like Will, I was just starting to realize that I might not be straight, and I struggled to separate what it meant to have a disease from what it meant to be different from my classmates for this other reason. They got jumbled together in my head in ways that took a long time to untangle.

Now, I understand that being gay is absolutely *not* a disease. I wouldn't change that part of myself for anything, even if there are some things about the world I would love to change. And while, as of the writing of this book, there is still no cure for Crohn's disease (hopefully *that* will change soon!), I now understand that my illness is just one part of me. I am so much more. With routine checkups, self-care, and medicines, I am able to keep my disease under control.

Every person with inflammatory bowel diseases like Crohn's and colitis has their own unique story to tell. Recent estimates put the total number around 6 to 8 million people living with IBD around the world, and yet no two experiences are exactly alike. But for all of us, the stigma surrounding these diseases can make seeking help and getting treatment that much scarier. The symptoms can seem embarrassing, especially when you're a kid.

Please know this: if you are struggling with any kind of chronic illness, it is not your fault. If anyone tries to make you feel bad for being different in any way, that's on them—not you. You are perfect just the way you are. And you shouldn't have to wait to feel like you belong.

ADDITIONAL RESOURCES

The Crohn's & Colitis Foundation:
www.crohnscolitisfoundation.org

Athletes vs. Crohn's & Colitis: *www.athletesvscrohns.org*

The Trevor Project: *www.thetrevorproject.org*

The American Civil Liberties Union: *www.aclu.org*

ACKNOWLEDGMENTS

Thank you to my editor, Rosemary Brosnan, who inspired me to write this book and then challenged me to write it better. I am honored to benefit from Rosemary's brilliant questions and insights. (And any shortfalls or oversights in the book are my own.)

Thank you to my agent, Sara Crowe, whose support and guidance mean the world.

Thank you to Courtney Stevenson, Jill Amack, Laura Harshberger, and all the folks at Quill Tree/HarperCollins who've helped this book along in its publication journey.

Thank you to designer David Curtis and artist Mojo Wang for working their magic on the cover art for this book.

Thank you to Jess MacLeish and Alex Arnold. Our virtual check-ins got this book and me both through the winter of 2021, and I am forever grateful for that.

Thank you to David Levithan, Nico Medina, Billy Merrell, Mike Ross, and Nick Eliopulos for listening to an early chapter and encouraging me on. And Nick, thank you for saving me from my lapses in video game knowledge.

Thank you to the doctors (and there have been many!) who've helped me navigate life with a chronic illness. I have to give special thanks to Dr. Chip, Dr. Schoen, and Dr. Jacob. I can't imagine what my life would look like without these doctors in it, and I am so very fortunate that my path crossed with theirs.

Finally, thank you to my family—Mom, Dad, Terri, Kelly, Nick—for accompanying me to countless appointments and seeing me through all the ups and downs. Your love is the constant that has kept them all in balance.